"Tonight…when tha[...]
I thought at first tha[...]
She looked at him. [...]
looked at him. "You're in my heart, Kerry.
You're there. Exactly where you've always
been. As much as you've always been. I
just need you to know that."

For a brief second, her spirit soared. She was young
again. With a heart filled with hope and possibility.
With plans. With a heart that knew how to dream. And
then reality hit. Him standing there in his expensive
clothes. In front of a wall filled with her brother's
murder details.

She wasn't the only one who'd been hurt by Rafe's
defection. And he hadn't said a word about coming
back, either. About being friends in the future.

Because he couldn't. She got that. He'd been a
Colton for too long. His family depended on him. And
he on them, too, she figured. Whether he liked that or
not.

She wanted to tell him that he was in her heart, too,
but that door wasn't open. Not even a little bit.

* * *

Book two of the Coltons of Mustang Valley

* * *

Dear Reader,

I'm thrilled to have you join me for book two of The Coltons of Mustang Valley! I love being part of this family, and I hope you feel like you are one of us!

I was an introvert and pretty much a loner growing up. Definitely not one of the popular kids. So when I was asked to tell the story of a woman who'd lost the love of her life because she wasn't "good enough," I knew I was up to the task. I love Kerry. She's had some truly tough times, but she doesn't let them define her. She doesn't let them victimize her. Instead, she finds her own strength and creates a life that she loves. And Rafe... Oh, my word, the heir who isn't really one of them, but gives his whole life to trying... He's one of those heroes you just take with you when you go.

I hope you'll enjoy the Colton family as much as the family that is bringing them to you has done so. It takes a tribe to create stories like these, and all of us involved with the Coltons form a bond, working together, during the year it takes us to bring these people to life. We're very, very happy to have you become a part of us.

Tara Taylor

COLTON'S LETHAL REUNION

Tara Taylor Quinn

Tara Taylor Quinn

HARLEQUIN®ROMANTIC SUSPENSE

Special thanks and acknowledgment are given to
Tara Taylor Quinn for her contribution to
The Coltons of Mustang Valley miniseries.

Recycling programs
for this product may
not exist in your area.

ISBN-13: 978-1-335-62637-0

Colton's Lethal Reunion

Copyright © 2020 by Harlequin Books S.A.

This edition published by arrangement with Harlequin Books S.A.

For questions and comments about the quality of this book, please contact us at CustomerService@Harlequin.com.

Printed in U.S.A.

www.Harlequin.com

Having written over eighty-five novels, **Tara Taylor Quinn** is a *USA TODAY* bestselling author with more than seven million copies sold. She is known for delivering intense, emotional fiction. Tara is a past president of Romance Writers of America and is a seven-time RWA RITA® Award finalist. She has also appeared on TV across the country, including *CBS Sunday Morning*. She supports the National Domestic Violence Hotline. If you need help, please contact 1-800-799-7233.

Books by Tara Taylor Quinn

Visit the Author Profile page at
Harlequin.com for more titles.

For Rachel Marie. I think of you in all I do and have been reminded through this book that family is forever—the tie that binds is too strong to break. I love you.

Chapter 1

He had to see her. This wasn't news. Rafe Colton had known for years that he owed Kerry Wilder an explanation for the way he'd cut out on her—on them—abandoning her and their budding love with no warning. Leaving her to face life alone after they'd been friends, best friends, even secret friends, since they'd been old enough to walk and talk.

For years he'd known. And for years, he'd been avoiding her.

For so many reasons. Not the least of which was that he suspected, maybe even feared, that he was still in love with her. He couldn't be, of course. There was no way the pubescent feelings of youth would carry unrequited into adulthood. And certainly wouldn't still be incubating in a grown man of thirty-six.

And yet, he'd procrastinated. Which made him not real fond of himself—deep down in the places he rarely visited, at least.

And then, in the middle of the shock that had rocked his whole adoptive family—the Coltons—she'd walked in the room. And in the two days since, he'd been able to think of little else. Payne, his adoptive father, had been shot—was still lying comatose, unchanged since he'd been admitted to the hospital—his oldest brother was the prime suspect in the murder, and Kerry was the detective assigned to the case.

How could that possibly be?

Okay, he knew how. At eighteen, Kerry had left the ranch where they'd both grown up, but she'd returned to Mustang Valley after college. Had joined the police force in the small Arizona town that was home to Colton Oil. As far as he knew, she hadn't been near Rattlesnake Ridge Ranch since. Probably didn't know that, unlike the biological Colton heirs, he'd moved out of the family mansion he'd moved into at five, when he'd been orphaned and subsequently adopted by Payne and his first wife, Tessa.

Kerry also wouldn't know that, instead of moving back into the old foreman's house he'd lived in until his father had died—which, as a Colton, and CFO of Colton Oil, would have been completely inappropriate—he'd built his own home. The adopted, nonbiological Colton house. Sitting on a stretch of land out of view of the mansion, a flat piece on the other side of a hill close by the barns—the place where he and Kerry used to go play until he was no longer just the foreman's son and they weren't allowed to be seen together anymore. Then it was the place where they hid out, just to be able to see each other.

None of which mattered as the long stretch of two-lane road he'd been traveling through the barren and stark Arizona land gave way to signs of the town ahead. What mattered was that he had to see Kerry.

It wasn't a mistake that she'd been assigned to investigate his adopted father's attempted murder. It was fate. Forcing him to do what he should have done long ago. Especially since his adoptive brother Ace, who'd recently been outed as a non-Colton by blood, appeared to be a person of interest to her.

Giving him an excuse to go see her, to talk to her, without raising any eyebrows. Or Payne Colton's ire. Spoken displeasure, clear lessons that had held Rafe in check where Kerry was concerned for far too many years.

The last admission made him slightly sick. He wasn't thirteen anymore, ashamed after being caught during his first kiss. He was a man who should have known better then to have let so much time pass. Who should have come clean sooner.

Or at the very least, apologized.

She could look at the video for the hundredth time. Study it another few hours and still come up with no more than she already knew. Payne Colton's elegant and luxurious corner office showed up in black-and-white on the security footage. And a tad bit grainy. Made the looking easier for her without the proof of his lavish living so obvious. And identifying his shooter more difficult.

She knew what she knew—very little and not enough—
and all the staring in the world wasn't changing that.

"Kerry! You got a visitor."

James Donovan, the redheaded officer ten years her
junior, was leaning back in his chair to peer into the
small office Kerry shared with the department's only
other senior detective, P. J. Doherty. Why Doherty
couldn't have pulled the Colton case she didn't know,
but there you had it. Kerry was stuck with it. Spencer
was a sergeant, but he was also a Colton. Just a distant
cousin, and not close with his family, but also not appropriate for him to be working the case.

Standing, she nodded to Donovan, shut down her
screen, headed out front, and a so-so day got a whole
lot worse.

Rafe Colton. CFO of Colton Oil. The boy who'd
once been a lowly farmhand kid, like her, on the
Colton family's Rattlesnake Ridge Ranch.

With a backward look at Donovan, letting him
know she didn't appreciate him not giving her any
warning, she walked to the small reception area.

Donovan didn't know about her past with Rafe—as
far as she knew, no one did. But he should have given
her a heads-up that a member of the Colton family
was there. Especially since he'd just been involved in
a Colton case himself—helping catch a stalker who'd
been after another sibling, Marlowe.

It wasn't like they handled cases involving billion-
aires all that often. Or ever. And while the Coltons
weren't the only wealthy family within fifty miles of
sleepy little Mustang Valley, they were by far the most

prominent. The Colton heir, Ace, was her prime suspect at the moment.

"Mr. Colton." For anyone else, she'd have held out a hand in greeting. "What can I do for you?"

His head tilted a bit, as though her formal response to his sudden presence in her sphere surprised him. Whatever.

"Can we go someplace and talk?" While his body had changed enormously since the last time she'd stood close to him—filled out, sprouted up—his hair was still the thick blond mass she used to imagine running her fingers through. And those blue eyes... They looked right into her.

"No." She realized the inappropriateness of the stark response a second too late. "Not really," she amended. His dark pants, white shirt and tie were all new to her, but fitting for one who'd traded her away for a chance at having finer things. "I assume this is about your father's case?"

The word *father* stuck in her throat, but she got it out. Payne Colton might be Rafe's adoptive dad, but Kerry had known Rafe's biological father, Carter Kay. Known and loved him, probably as much as Rafe had. The man had taken Kerry's own father under his wing, and Kerry and her younger brother, too, because they were a package deal.

Carter had been foreman of Rattlesnake Ridge when Kerry's ranch hand father had been at his lowest point, recovering from the defection of his young wife, struggling to raise two young kids on his own. Tyler Wilder Sr. had been a hard worker until the day he'd died after falling thirty feet into an old grown-over mine in the desert. He'd also been a heavy drinker—mostly when he wasn't working, which didn't bode well for Kerry or Tyler Jr.'s home life. He didn't hit them or scream at them much. He was just too drunk to parent, and sometimes so drunk he needed to be parented. He'd stumble and break things. Said he'd take them places they needed to be, but then couldn't. Couldn't always even remember to pay all the bills.

"Please, Kerry, can we talk?"

Again, she shook her head, standing tall and slender in her jeans, oxford shirt and cowboy boots. If she'd known he was coming she'd have done more that morning than throw her long auburn hair—her best trait—up into a ponytail. *Ha.* If she'd known he was coming, she'd have made an excuse not to be there.

"I don't have much to tell you," she said. "Until or unless your…father…comes out of his coma and can answer some questions…"

Not entirely true. The shooter wasn't going to get away with attempted homicide. Or murder if Payne Colton didn't pull through. Even if she couldn't personally stand the man—or his adopted son.

The chief wasn't in, but two of their three full-time officers were busy behind her. They'd have no reason to pay attention to her discussion with a member of the victim's family. Unless they, like Rafe, were enamored with the Colton money.

"I've been over the security footage from your father's office," she offered, mostly to get rid of him. "The shooter can mostly just be seen in shadow and is hunched, so it's hard to tell much other than he or she is dressed all in black and is wearing a ski-type mask. We don't have an accurate height measurement of the body, only of the projectile of the bullet. Don't really even know if it's male or female, or have any idea of age. Just know that whoever did this is of a lean build. Maybe thin and the clothes add a little weight, but definitely not heavy."

Sliding his hands in his pockets, Rafe studied her with that potent gaze, and then said, "But you suspect Ace anyway, even though you have no real evidence against him. Because, what, he's not overweight?"

Okay, good. He was going to let the past go and just play his Colton part, as she was insisting he do. There was no reason for her to be disappointed by that. Or in him.

She didn't care enough.

"I have to consider what I do know," she said, ready to show him that while she might not be impressive enough for him in the personal department, she was a damned good detective. One of the best. "His whole life as he's known it has just been snatched away from him—something we call a stressor. He just finds out he's not really a Colton and then he threatens…your… Payne, in front of witnesses, telling him he'd regret having just removed Ace as CEO of your billion-dollar company. He admitted to me that he'd made the threat. He had access to Payne's private office here in town. And has no way to corroborate his alibi."

"He was at home, in his wing at the mansion, from eight o'clock on—dealing with work he brought home with him."

So Rafe had become a puppet for the man he now called brother. Spouting family speak.

"Security cameras don't bear testimony to that. Yet they show two of your other siblings coming in just before nine. You and Asher." If Rafe had been a suspect, she'd have had to recuse herself from the case. Too bad he wasn't.

"The system was probably on a momentary lag—it happens. Being set in the middle of thousands of acres of cattle ranch, it's not like the reception out there is perfect. And in the evenings, when most of the ranch hands are in their cabins using the internet, rather than out working, service can get a little sketchy."

Because, of course, the Coltons had the fancy, wireless camera system, not some independent job with a tape you could actually remove and take with you.

"And I suppose you'll use that same excuse to explain why there was no digital time stamp to verify that he'd been signed on at home, or to show any work he'd done?"

"He was going over employee files, ones that had been flagged from a recent performance review. He was looking at the physical files, signed documentation, which is why he was doing it at home. He didn't want anyone walking in on him."

Which was exactly what Ace and his attorney had told her. Didn't mean it was true. Only that the family had their story straight.

If only she had some solid forensic evidence, but there were so many people in and out of Payne's office; they'd found fibers and hairs from a number of people, including Ace, which meant little since he worked there. Rafe did, too. As did other siblings.

If only Ace hadn't insisted on having his lawyer

present when she'd questioned him the other night, she might have been able to get more out of him.

"Your *brother* sure didn't tamp down his anger when he was here the other night," she told Rafe, stumbling over that last word as she met his gaze head on. She'd shown him a dent in her armor and felt like she'd let herself down.

"How would you feel if there'd just been an attempt on your father's life, you're dragged away from the hospital where he's lying in a coma, from the rest of your family, and treated like a suspect?"

She wouldn't know. Her father hadn't been murdered. But her brother had. Not that anyone believed her about that yet. Another case she had to solve.

One she was actively working, albeit secretly, and determined to prove.

"Do you want whoever shot Payne to be caught and pay for what he or she did?" She looked him straight in the eye—to show him she could. That he had no hold over her whatsoever.

"Of course."

"Then you need to let me do my job," she told him. "And that means I look at every possibility and talk to anyone and everyone for whom I have questions."

Which didn't include him.

Although she could see him siding with Ace. Sympathizing with him. After all, now neither of them were able to hold the coveted CEO position of Colton Oil, since neither of them were biological Coltons.

"Kerry, please, I want to…"

She shook her head. Glanced at the small, big box store watch her father and brother had bought her for her sixteenth birthday. Her dad had forgotten to get a battery and had been too drunk to drive the ten miles into town to get one. Since she hadn't been allowed to take her driving test yet, and Tyler was only eleven, she'd worn the watch for almost a week before it actually told the correct time.

It hadn't been wrong since.

"I really have to get back, Mr. Colton," she said. "This case isn't going to solve itself and I'm the only detective working on it. I'll be sure to call your stepmother as soon as I have anything to share with you all."

Maybe she should have asked him how Payne was doing. She already knew. She'd called the hospital that morning to hear that there'd been no change in the older man. Each day he remained in a coma had to lessen his chances of coming out of it. Asking still would have been polite.

And had it been any other Colton...

Turning, she left Rafe standing there, her back ramrod straight as she walked, feeling the heat of his gaze all over her body.

He'd had more to say. She'd read his intent.

Had seen the sorrow in his gaze. The regret.

And absolutely could not stand there and take it.

Sometimes, no matter how much someone might have to offer, it really was too little, too late.

Chapter 2

A smart man would cut his losses. Tuck the regret so far away it would eventually fade into oblivion. Do whatever it took to help his family through both crisis and tragedy: one followed by the other in the space of mere hours.

He was the financial wizard. The one they all looked to for levelheaded, clear thinking. The mathematician who could figure out the way to make everything add up.

But nothing was adding up.

DNA proving that Ace wasn't a Colton? It made no sense. Seriously, a baby getting switched at birth? A sick one for a healthy one? No formula was going to be able to calculate that one.

And to think, even for a second, that Ace was capable of shooting Payne? Sure, he'd been pissed that

Payne had removed him as CEO, but he'd also known that killing Payne wasn't going to help his cause any. Payne had only been following Colton Oil bylaws, appointing a CEO who was a biological Colton, to protect the company. It hadn't been about Ace, but about keeping their billions safe. He knew Ace wanted that as badly as any of them. Would have stepped down himself if he'd been given a few days to come to terms with everything. Ace lived for Colton Oil and was surely more pissed at the fact that his whole life had been stolen from him, pissed at whoever had switched him at birth, pissed at fate.

And, as far as Rafe could see, Ace adored Payne Colton, if such a thing were possible.

Rafe had never found it so, in spite of the years he'd spent trying.

So what was it about him that drove him to give himself impossible tasks? To set himself up for emotional failure? Because that was certainly what he was doing, knowingly doing, as he parked his fancy new metallic navy blue truck out in front of Kerry's small, but nicely landscaped stucco home that afternoon before heading back to the ranch.

His own, much more opulent home was waiting for him. It was full of food brought over by one of the mansion staff and left in his refrigerator, as was procedure any night that he didn't present himself at the family table for dinner. And whether he made it back to the ranch on time that night or not, he wasn't going to dinner. The staff had always spoiled him. Possibly because when Tessa Ainsley Colton died, his upbringing had been largely left to those running the household.

Payne's first wife was the only reason Rafe had become a Colton. Carter had been such a vital part of their lives for so long, had lost his wife right there on the ranch from valley fever, and Tessa Colton had insisted that the family take in Rafe. Payne had argued with her about it, which he wasn't supposed to know, and no one knew he knew. He'd gone to see Tessa one night and had heard them. And had gone back to his room and cried himself to sleep. He'd worried about what was going to happen to him and then, suddenly, he was told he was going to be a Colton. Obviously, Payne had eventually given in. Then Tessa had died and Payne's second wife, Selina, hadn't given a rat's ass about the little orphaned boy.

He wasn't even sure how many of the siblings would be at dinner that night. They were taking shifts sitting with Payne at the hospital. He'd done his stint before going to see Kerry that morning.

A light was on in her front window, though it was only four in the afternoon. The garage door was shut. There were no vehicles in the driveway. He didn't pull in. Leaving his parked truck at the curb, he approached the front door. She could still refuse to talk to him. He wouldn't blame her.

She could threaten him with a restraining order if he didn't leave her alone. It wasn't like she'd have to call the cops. She *was* the cop.

And still, he lifted his hand to knock.

She'd been over the files again and again. Had a wall in her dining room covered with a huge ten-year calendar, chronicling her brother's life from the time he'd graduated high school until his death. All of the jobs he'd had were marked with color-coded dots for the months or years he'd worked them. The bills he'd paid, banking transactions, times when she'd found nothing to account for his whereabouts. No credit card charges because he hadn't had any cards. And she only had phone calls from logging into his account because she hadn't had a warrant.

Next to the calendar was a smaller one, covering the two-year span before Tyler's death. It showed what she could find of the activity of Odin Rogers, a slick local criminal who had his hands in many dirty dealings— seriously dirty, Kerry suspected, like drug running and maybe weapons, too. Yet he managed to always skate free of any charges against him. Also, in color-coded dots, she'd marked the phone calls and known meetings between her brother and the slimeball. Odin had had some kind of hold on Tyler. She figured it had to do with Tyler's earlier, druggie days.

Those phone calls and meetings lasted several months, before Tyler had supposedly committed suicide by falling off a cliff. The calendar showed only two colored marks. One the same week that Tyler had sworn to her that he was straightening out his life, and the other one early in the morning on the day he'd died.

The day Odin Rogers had had him murdered. She was sure of the truth. Just could not find the evidence to prove it. To get justice for Tyler…

A loud rapping interrupted her focus. She'd thought she'd heard a knock, but had ignored the summons. She was on her own time now, and as much as she loved her town, her job, there were times when the well-meaning citizens of Mustang Valley needed to get along without her. After seeing Rafe earlier in the day, that evening was definitely one of those times.

While she hadn't changed out of the jeans and oxford she'd worn to work, she'd pulled the elastic out of her hair on her way to an eventual hot soak with lavender-scented candles and bath beads before dinner. Pouring on the calm. She'd gotten distracted on her way through the dining room, though.

Still, whoever was out there was being persistent, so of course she had to take a peek. The chief would have called her if there was anything urgent. As would anyone else from the department. An intruder wouldn't announce themselves so boldly…

Rafe. Still in the clothes he'd been wearing when he'd descended upon her that morning.

Shaking, hating the sudden feeling of being afraid of herself, she froze there by the window, able to see him without him knowing she was looking. If she waited long enough, he'd go away. He'd have no other option. And no way of knowing for sure that she was in the house.

He frowned. Shook his head. Glanced at his watch. Stared at her front door. Then looked toward the sky.

No. It had to be coincidence. Or something that had just become habit without any correlation to anything that had once meant something.

He did not just implore their mothers to help them.

He'd looked up. That was all. Had certainly long forgotten the ritual they'd made up together when they were six or seven and meeting on the other side of the hill that backed up to the RRR barns. They and Tyler—who was five years younger, still a baby when

Kerry's mom had taken off—were the only mother-
less kids on the ranch. They were best friends. And a
year or two earlier, Payne and Tessa had adopted Rafe.
Since the day he was adopted at five, Payne had forbidden Rafe to have anything to do with Kerry. But
they'd sneaked away anyway. Knowing that if their
birth moms were still alive, like the rest of the kids,
the mothers would have made sure they still got to play
together. They'd look to the sky and ask their moms to
not let them get caught by Payne. And for eight years,
their pleas had been answered.

Of course, that was back before Rafe knew the
value of the Colton dollar. And before she'd known
that her mom was in Phoenix, more interested in drugs
and men than any children she'd birthed.

When Rafe's chin lowered, he glanced at the window. For a second she was afraid he saw her. And then
saw herself. Saw how ridiculous she was being.

She was a thirty-six-year-old police detective, not
a thirteen-year-old virgin having her first kiss. And
had long since rid her heart of Rafe Colton. She had
nothing to hide. Not even from herself.

With that thought in mind, she pulled open the front
door.

Kerry didn't look happy to see him. He didn't blame
her. Hadn't expected any different.

"Can I come in?"

"No."

He nodded. "I'm more ashamed than I can say that
it took Payne's attempted murder to bring me to the
point of seeking you out," he said. She wasn't likely to

give him a second chance to explain. Or much time, either. "I've known for years, ever since you got back, that I had to speak to you, to explain…"

Her brows rose, her long, auburn hair trailing down around her shoulders, just as he remembered it. When he was twelve, he'd worked up the guts to tell her he liked it that way. That had been a tough year for him—noticing her as a girl, not just a friend. Wanting to be more than just friends, but having no clue what that even meant in any practical sense.

"I didn't expect you'd have noticed," she said. He paid close attention to the words. They didn't say a whole lot—and yet, they said so much more than he deserved.

There were chinks in her armor. He'd hoped, for a second that morning, that he'd witnessed one of those chinks, but she'd recovered so quickly he hadn't been sure.

"I have always noticed everything about you," he said. Like the fact that she'd just looked past his shoulder toward the street. He'd heard a car go by. Someone she knew?

"You shouldn't have parked that fancy truck of yours out front," she said. "People will talk."

"More so if we're standing out here on your porch," he told her, a weak attempt to get into her house. To see her space, to be able to picture it, to have a real conversation with her.

Nodding, she stood back, held open the door. "But you aren't staying, Rafe," she told him. "You can say whatever it is you feel compelled to say, but then you go. And you don't come back."

"You're the one with the weapon, Detective," he

said. "I left my rifle in its case on the floor of my truck…" He was pretty sure there'd been some pithy follow-up on the tip of his tongue, but all thought vanished as he caught his first scent of her space. His first view.

And felt like he'd come home.

"I'd apologize for furniture that comes from a discount home store, and rugs that are polyester blend, instead of the real wool you're used to," Kerry said, standing on the four-by-six area of tile that led from the front door into her living room. "But I'm sure you knew what to expect when you came slumming." *Shut up. Shut up. Shut up.*

She felt like a gutter rat, standing there with him consuming her house just by stepping in the door.

"And hey, I give you credit…you didn't waste much time seeking me out once Payne was safely in a coma and so unlikely to catch you mixing with the help."

The Help. She imagined it with a capital *H*. Like it was a name. God, she hated those words. The Help. Had heard it far too many times, in her own head, as she'd cried herself to sleep, night after night. Year after year. Not every night. Not all year. But far too often.

She'd hadn't been on the ranch to *help* anyone. She'd been a kid. Growing up, like any other kid had a right to do.

She hated him for abiding by those social rules, letting those words destroy the most valuable thing in her life.

"If I was going to stop hanging out with you because I thought you were beneath me, I'd have done it when I was five," he said. "Or six, or seven, or eight."

Did he think she hadn't already tried to give him that benefit of the doubt? That she hadn't spent years trying to understand?

"You didn't yet know what Colton money could buy you."

"Of course I did," he said. "I knew that the first night I slept in the mansion. Even at five, my pajamas were silk and the sheets were softer than anything I'd ever felt before. I had a huge bed, and a room full of new toys waiting for me."

He'd never told her that. "You said the pajamas were cold."

"They were. But I liked how they felt. I never felt like you were beneath me, Kerry. Not ever. To the contrary, I felt like I was a lowlife, ditching you like I did."

She might have believed that ten—twenty—years before. Back when she'd still been foolish enough to hope that adulthood would free them to be together.

But if telling her his fanciful version of the truth got him out of her house, of her life, quicker, then she was all ears. "So why did you? Ditch me?"

"Because I was madly in love with you. And thirteen. When Payne caught us kissing... I was...hard... and embarrassed and I freaked out. How could I be in love? I was only thirteen. But you...you were like a siren or something, calling me to you. The strength of those feelings scared me. It wasn't like I had anyone to talk to about it. But Payne had plenty to say about the kinds of boys who fooled around with the help. And what that did to the girls they fooled around with, too..."

She couldn't let his words sink inside her, couldn't

let them get to that deep private place she no longer accessed. Didn't even want them in her head. But there they were. Before she saw their danger, they'd already made their way between her ears. Couldn't allow herself to feel *anything* for that thirteen-year-old boy who'd been so lonely in that big house with all the important people.

And so alone in the world.

She'd had Tyler. And her dad, who, while drunk most evenings, had always been clear in his love for his children. And in his desire to be there for them. He'd been a kind drunk. A strong worker. And a weak man.

Rafe had been made to act like a man at five.

Not that it changed anything. He'd been grown for a long time since then. Had had more than a decade with her back in town and not once had he made any attempt to seek her out. Not to apologize. Explain. Give any indication to her that she'd mattered at all. Not even when Tyler had died…

"What is all this?"

He'd seen "the wall." When she'd let him in, she hadn't even thought about the small part of the L-shaped living/dining area in her home. She'd only thought about not wanting anyone who knew her seeing her talking to Rafe Colton on her doorstep.

Hadn't been able to bear the thought of having to answer questions.

Hadn't wanted to bear the shame, even secretly inside, of knowing that she'd once ranked Rafe Colton at the very top of her list of loved ones. Ahead even of Tyler and her dad. Only to be cast off because she was "the help."

The truck outside, she could find a way to explain. If she had to. The Coltons weren't the only guys in Arizona who drove cool trucks. Expensive trucks.

"So, can you tell me what this is about?" Rafe was frowning as he moved along the wall, reading, she assumed.

"A case I'm working on," she told him. "A cold case."

Tyler wasn't named on the wall.

Neither was Odin.

Rafe studied details anyway. And then turned around to see the folders on the table. Tyler's name was big and bold right on top.

"I was told his death was an accident."

Or a suicide. Both theories had spread through town. Officially it had been ruled an accident.

"He was murdered," she told him, feeling like a traitor for even sharing that much with Rafe. She wasn't the only one who'd suffered when Rafe deserted them. Tyler had idolized his older sister's friend. Had been bereft without Rafe's support, and what he'd viewed as Rafe's protection.

"The school year after that last…summer, he was starting fourth grade," she said aloud. Maybe for Tyler. Maybe because it just had to be said. "Being little for his age hadn't been an issue in third grade. A lot of guys were still small. But by fourth grade, kids started picking on him. He came home all bloodied up one day and just kept saying, 'I gotta tell Rafe, he'll make 'em stop.'"

She could hear the words as clearly that night as

the day they'd been said. "I had to physically hold him back from running up to the mansion to find you."

She'd never been sure what Tyler thought Rafe could have done, even if he'd still been their friend. Since Rafe was older, it wasn't like he was ever on Tyler's elementary school campus.

But that had been the year that changed her little brother. He might not have been as big as the other boys, but he'd been smart. And he'd toughened up. By seventh grade he'd been running with the trouble-makers who'd once made fun of him. Running *them*.

By the time she'd come home from college in Phoenix, he'd been running drugs, too, though she never got him to admit that. And he'd never been caught. She saw the money in his room, though.

And saw him getting high and drunk every night.

She'd been away getting an education, attending the police academy to make their little world a safer place for people without Rafes to protect them, and while she'd been gone, he'd turned into her father.

"He fell off a cliff, right?" Rafe was going through photos, having opened the folder without seeking permission first. So Colton-ish.

"He was driven up there and pushed off."

He looked at her—studied her, more like it. "You sound sure about that."

"I am sure. I just don't have the evidence to prove it. Yet."

"He was pulled off the mountain drunk more than once," Rafe said softly, compassion in his gaze.

"How do you know that?"

"Because while you were gone…he was in high

school…I made sure that he got back to the ranch, to your cabin, without Payne ever hearing about it."

She'd wondered how Tyler had been so wild without being kicked off the ranch. He'd left on his own. After he'd graduated from high school.

"I made sure he stayed until he graduated," Rafe added.

"I don't believe that. Tyler would have said something…"

"He didn't know. I…had a talk with one of the guys in your department, Spencer… The police made a deal with Tyler that he wouldn't be charged with underage drinking as long as he stayed in school. And they watched over him, just happening to show up wherever he might be getting himself into trouble."

Wow. Just… Wow.

What did you do with that piece of information?

How did you hate a guy who…

Not that you liked him, again, too much else had happened…

He'd looked after Tyler while she'd been gone. Had made sure her brother got his education.

She just couldn't believe it.

Wished she'd known. And it still wasn't enough. Didn't make up for ditching them in the first place. For choosing wealth over love.

Because even if, as a kid, he'd felt he had no choice, five years after that last ultimatum, he'd been an adult. And yet he'd waited twenty-three years…

Seriously, what did you do with something like that?

Chapter 3

Rafe studied the information about Tyler's death so he didn't have to look at Kerry. Or feel her home around him, reminding him of everything he'd once had and never found again. Not the room. Or the furnishings. It was a sense of being fully and completely alive.

She hadn't said a word since he'd broken his promise to himself and told her what he'd done for Tyler while she'd been at the police academy. He'd gone away to college, too, but he'd had a helicopter that brought him home for three days every weekend. Payne's insistence. His way to keep control, Rafe had figured. "Why are you so certain that this wasn't an accident?" he finally asked, closing the folder when he couldn't bear to look at the pictures any longer. The cliff face. The tire tracks and footprints in the dust.

The funeral he'd missed because he'd been at an international oil summit in Washington with a couple of his siblings—or the biological Colton heirs, as he sometimes thought of them. Although, why she had a picture of the people gathered at the grave site...

He glanced again. Noticed the man standing in the back of the small gathering. And then looked at the wall again. And through another file. "You think Odin Rogers had something to do with this?"

The man was little more than a scumbag with no morals, no class, who lived like a member of royalty—thinking his word and desires carried the weight of a king. He'd tried to take on Rafe once—when Rafe had been looking out for Tyler. Not face-to-face, of course. But word got around that the Coltons couldn't save Tyler if the punk didn't finish some job for which he'd been paid. No job that was on any record, of course. It hadn't ended well for Rogers. And yet, the hefty white man continued to live well. And free.

Rogers's one success was that he had enough minions willing to do his dirty work so that his hands were clean when it came to actual proof of dealing drugs.

"I know he's behind it," Kerry said, standing to join him by the wall. "I know Tyler got into trouble, that he made some horrible choices there for a while..." She paused and Rafe felt the sting of guilt, whether she'd intended it or not. "But he was on the straight and narrow for almost a year before he was murdered. I know that he'd been running with some of Odin's people. I saw him downtown, talking to Odin once, but when I asked him about it, he denied knowing the guy. Kept trying to convince me that I'd seen it wrong.

Then something went down that either scared him, or opened his eyes to what he was becoming, because he came to me and apologized for all the worry and trouble he'd brought me over the years. He told me that he knew how much I'd done for him, that I was always there for him. Told me how much that meant to him. And he swore that he was going to make it all up to me…"

She'd been sounding all police-like…until she didn't. Her voice didn't break, it just trailed off. And she stared unmoving at the wall.

Collecting herself, Rafe knew. Not because it was anything she'd ever done around him before; on the contrary, she'd always shown him everything she was feeling, when they were kids. But he knew she wasn't going to let herself show him anything, anymore.

The practical adult man he'd grown into was glad about that. Because if Payne lived, and Rafe truly hoped he did, the old man would likely still carry through on his threats to a thirteen-year-old Rafe. Back then all he'd have had to do was fire her father. Which would have been akin to sending Kerry and Tyler straight into hell. With Tyler Sr.'s drinking, the kids would likely have been left to fend for themselves. Or become wards of the state, and risk being split up. At least on the ranch they were always looked after by the other cowboys' wives. And Tyler was looked after, too, by the men who trusted him to work hard come morning. At the RRR they could be together as a family. And one thing Rafe had always known was how much Kerry loved her little brother. And her father, too.

But even now that Rafe and Kerry were adults, Payne could wield his power. Have Kerry pressured out of the Mustang Valley Police department, forcing her to leave the town that had been her home her entire life to seek out other employment. The man meant well—he was fiercely loyal and loved his family—but he also believed that he knew best and used his power to see that his will was done.

And he believed that where Kerry Wilder was concerned, Rafe was weak. Or he just held a grudge because Rafe had managed to carry on a secret friendship with her for eight years before the man found out.

Either way, Rafe wasn't going to be the cause of that power being unleashed on Kerry.

"There has to be a reason that he was up on that mountain." Kerry's words, calm and professional again, broke into his thoughts. "That's not where he ever climbed, or hung out. There's nothing up there. Not even a good view. And the tire tracks don't match his car," she added. "They're bigger, the tread is wider."

"So what's the official explanation for that?"

She shrugged. "There's no proof that those tire tracks had anything to do with Tyler's death. Someone could have been up there before, or after he went over. As dry as it was, they could have been there for a couple of days. And there's no proof that anyone else was with him. You see the footprints…there are several partials, different shoes…so we know people were up there, but not necessarily when he was. The theory is that it was a new hangout spot, but no one has come forward saying so. Or admitting to having been up there. And it's not like there's a surveillance camera…

"If it hadn't been for a hiker finding his body down below, we would likely never have known what happened to him…"

"How long was he down there?"

"A couple of days." She shook her head. Studied the wall as though the answer was there for her to see. And maybe it was. She seemed so certain. He followed her gaze.

"It could be that the prints in the photo were from people who heard about his death and went up to look," she continued, "but there's got to be evidence there, too. He was up there. We know that. I need to know why. Because I am certain he didn't climb a mountain and jump. Or go hiking and fall off. There was no evidence of him having slid off, no ground broken away, no sign of a body hitting the sides, or sliding, on the way down."

"So let's go back and take another look." Rafe didn't think before he spoke. But didn't regret the words.

Kerry stared at him. "What?"

He looked her straight in the eye. "Look, I know some of the responsibility for this lies on me. I knew he looked up to me, and I just quit his life. Let me at least do this. Let me help. I've got an analytical mind. And fresh eyes. I've never been up there. So take me up. Show me. Maybe I'll notice something that wouldn't appear significant to someone trained to assess a crime scene."

"It's been two years…"

"But maybe something up there will trigger an

idea…a possibility you haven't yet thought of. I really want to help, Kerry. If you never speak to me again after this, fine, I deserve that. But let me at least help you find justice for Tyler."

He knew he had her before she opened her mouth. He recognized the look in her eyes before she glanced away.

If he'd needed proof that what had once been sacred between them wasn't dead yet, he'd just had it.

And knew, just as he had twenty-three years before, that he was going to have to walk away from it.

Because sometimes the heart didn't win.

"It's still going to be light for another hour. Can you go now?" Kerry knew better than to let Rafe Colton back into her personal sphere—knew he'd be heading right back out again—but if he was willing to help her find justice for Tyler, she wanted to use him quickly and be done.

While she had to have dealings with him anyway because she'd been assigned his father's case.

No one else wanted anything to do with investigating Tyler's death. His case was done. Closed. They thought her paranoid, needing to get over it, at worst. And a grieving sister who was struggling to accept the truth, at best. Which was why the case files were at home, not work. Why her dining room wall had become an investigation board.

"I'm not really dressed for a trek up the mountain…" He looked at her and finished, "But, yeah, let's go now."

Whether he still had the talent to read her, or she'd

just been obvious in her thoughts of "now or never," she didn't care to guess. But after locking up, she holstered her gun at her waist and headed out of her house through the door off the kitchen that led to a two-car garage.

Rafe offered to drive. To take his truck. She wasn't riding anywhere with him. The control was all hers or she wasn't going.

Not that she said as much aloud. She just got in her Jeep and pushed the button to raise the garage door. He climbed in beside her without pressing the matter.

Smart man.

"One of the last times that Tyler talked about having changed his life around...he was telling me how good he was doing, loved working as a cowboy, actually out on the range for a week at a time, moving herds, running down strays and assisting with difficult births. He'd been thinking about riding in an amateur rodeo during the county fair...and then he let something slip," she said, doing everything she could to remain fully focused on the case at hand, and not getting distracting by the man at her side.

"He said that he was staying away from the 'Big B.' He paled right afterward and when I questioned him on it, he just shook his head."

"The Big B? Is that a person?"

"I have no idea, but I assume so. It kind of sounded like it, like it was someone he had to avoid, not a place he just didn't go to anymore. I've looked all over the county and can't find any establishment that would go by the name Big B."

"Odin Rogers doesn't have a *B*," Rafe said, almost as though she hadn't already figured *that* out.

"And his middle name is Paul," she let him know she'd done her homework. And could spell enough to know there was no *B* in that, either.

"I'm thinking that someone who works for Rogers is the Big B. Maybe one of his hired thugs. Or, I suppose, it could be some kind of moniker for a substance cocktail, but not one that's on any radar."

The entrance to the drive up the mountain was several miles outside of town, in the opposite direction from the RRR. The well-worn, if little used one-lane road had been carved into the mountain back in the early days of gold and copper mining. Her Jeep bounced up it just fine, taking the sometimes harrowing turns slowly when she couldn't see ahead to know if she'd need to yield to oncoming vehicles.

"You've obviously done this a few times," Rafe said, holding on to the handle just above the door frame. He didn't look nervous though. He was smiling.

And she almost missed the next turn.

Being up on the mountain with Rafe, away from the world, with only more mountains, higher peaks, and the gulch below in sight, threw her. They'd spent most of their hours together out in the middle of nowhere, out of view, out of sight, so they wouldn't be caught together. In the vast Arizona landscape, she'd felt so free.

Free from her father's drinking. From worry. From little Tyler needing things from her.

Free to love Rafe Kay.

Free to love Rafe Colton.

Standing up on that mountain with him, even several feet apart, watching him look over an area she pretty much knew by heart, she felt her whole being suffused with a sense of rightness, followed by a stream of longing that almost brought her to her knees. Everything about him was familiar in that moment. The way a few strands of his thick blond hair picked up when a breeze blew over them. The set of his shoulders. The intent focus he gave to whatever had his attention.

How could twenty-three years make no difference at all? Especially when it made all the difference in the world?

"This is where he went over," he said, apparently not as affected by being alone in the wilderness with her as she was with him. And why would he be? He'd probably taken a lot of girls back to their old hiding places. And why not? They were a known way to get past Payne.

Those old hiding places were all part of his family's land.

"Yes." She gave herself a strong mental shake and focused on why she was up on that mountain. On why she was talking to Rafe Colton at all.

"And there was no scuffle? No sign of struggle?"

She shook her head. Another fact that Chief Barco had taken into consideration before ruling her brother's death accidental.

"But if he was facing the gully down below, thinking he was alone, or if he was up here with someone he trusted, he could easily have been taken off guard."

Tyler could have been making out with someone.

Not that she'd ever considered that before, but she definitely knew how lost you could get in a kiss when you were out in the middle of nowhere…

"He hadn't been expecting to be in a fight. Hadn't had a chance to defend himself," she said, bringing her thoughts firmly back to current ground.

Rafe turned slowly, glancing all around them. He didn't walk far, didn't venture too close to the cliff's edge.

Glancing at the slick-bottomed, expensive leather dress shoes he was wearing, she didn't blame him.

"What's over there?" He motioned to a cliff side that tilted downward, toward another shallower gully off to the left of where Tyler had been pushed.

Shrugging, she walked that way. "I never climbed down to see," she said. It wasn't like she'd hiked an entire mountain range. Most particularly not alone. No reason to do so. "There's no path, no sign of broken vegetation, so obviously it's not a place people go." She moved closer, anyway. Rafe thought he noticed something.

She trusted his instincts.

Not him.

But he'd always had good instincts. Like the time he'd shoved her back and to the ground, a seemingly mean thing to do, until she'd noticed the rattlesnake he'd prevented her from stepping near. He noticed things. Knew things. He always had…

What the…

"Rafe, look…" She was probably just seeing things. "Is that a trail over there? Leading to that cliff face across the way?"

When he came up beside her, she turned red. Hot. Embarrassed that she'd just been seeing things. Of course there was no…

"I'm not sure," he said. "If it is, it's covered over with all of those tumbleweeds."

"Yeah." She'd been overreacting.

To him. Which clouded her normally spot-on thinking. She could feel his body heat. He was that close. And could smell him, too.

It wasn't possible that a boy of thirteen would carry the same scent as a man of thirty-six. Logically, she knew that. Her olfactory nerves were out of control.

"It's kind of funny, though, that they're all conglomerated around that one area, don't you think?" She had to say something, even if it was stupid. Better than standing there letting the past take control of her present. Ruin her present.

"Not if the wind blew them. They stopped there because of the cliff face…"

Something sounded behind them. A crunch of something heavy on the hard ground. Hand to her gun, Kerry froze. If it was a bear, or, more likely, a mountain lion, their greatest hope was to keep it calm. To pray that it didn't charge them before she could turn and get a shot off.

"What're you two doin' up 'ere?"

Not recognizing the voice, yet relieved to know that their intruder was human, Kerry spun around, her gun steady and pointing forward.

"Hey there…put that thing down. You ain't s'posed to be huntin' up here…"

The man was older than both of them by a good

ten years. Maybe more. Rough looking and wearing a forest ranger uniform. Dropping her gun, she reached into her back pocket for her badge wallet.

"I'm Detective Kerry Wilder," she said, aware of Rafe right behind her as she approached the man, showing him her identification.

"Yes'm, I know who you are," the man said, pulling out his own ID. "Grant Alvin," he said. "My wife and I transferred in with the Forest Service about five years ago. Used to be up at the Grand Canyon," he said.

Kerry knew some of the forest rangers in the area by sight. Not all. Those near Mustang Valley usually lived in remote, government housing, someplace in national forest territory. And unless there was a matter in MVPD's jurisdiction, they didn't really cross paths.

But if he'd been in the area for five years... Shouldn't someone have talked to him about Tyler's death? She hadn't seen his name in any reports. Getting excited as she faced a possible new lead, she said, "I'm investigating my brother's death." She named Tyler and gave the man the date and time of death that the coroner had given two years ago.

Staying silent, Rafe stood right beside her, like he was poised to jump to her defense at any moment. Fancy clothes and all. Like his slippery shoes would get anywhere near as far as her well-worn cowboy boots.

Still, she was glad he was there. If the ranger *had* been a bear—if she'd been about to die—having Rafe there, dying with him...

"You lookin' at that old case agin?" Alvin looked

at her like she was cow dung. "It was an accident. They all said so."

"Maybe it was," Kerry acknowledged, not wanting to get on the wrong side of the Forest Service. "I'd just like to be sure."

"Seems like there'd be more important stuff for you to be doin'," the somewhat-large man said, holding his ground, his arms crossed against his chest.

"I'm doing this in my own time," she told him. And then asked, "You said you've been in the area for five years."

"That's right."

"And you patrol this mountain?"

"Sometimes. Depends."

"Were you here two years ago?"

"Off and on."

"You ever notice any suspicious activity?"

"No."

Something about the speed of his response put her on edge. Further on edge. The guy seemed pissed off. Put out.

She and Rafe weren't doing anything wrong. The land was open to the public. They hadn't even veered far from where they'd pulled the Jeep off the track.

"No one hanging around…no vehicles that visit frequently? Anything that might be big enough to haul guns in and out? Repeat visitors who only stay a minute or two each time they come?"

"Nothin'," Alvin said, dropping his arms to take a step closer to them. "There's nothin'. And now the two of yous need to be getting on down the hill," he said. "It's getting late, gonna be dark soon, and there's all kind of wild animals out here at night. I sure don't want to be having to come back up and git you down," he said. And then, with a sour look added, "And them thousand-dollar leather shoes sure ain't gonna keep that one from sliding off a cliff." He practically spat the last four words.

Before either of them could respond, the man turned and then walked off.

Kerry could have called him back, but she was just as glad to see him go.

"What the hell was that?" she breathed, staring at Rafe. "Did he just threaten you?"

"Seemed that way." Eyes narrowed, Rafe was staring after Alvin, who'd apparently come upon them on foot. There was no other vehicle in the immediate vicinity, which would explain why they didn't know he'd been approaching.

"How'd he know we were up here?"

"I'm guessing he heard the Jeep. Came to check us out."

Which would be his job. Still… "He seemed kind of paranoid, though. What's it to him if I look into a cold case?"

"I'm not sure." Rafe didn't say much, but one look at his face told Kerry that he wasn't blowing off the incident. He was going to find out more.

Because he had the clout to do so.

And for the first time in a very, very long time, she was glad that she knew Rafe Colton.

Chapter 4

He knew exactly who to call. Chafing to get down off the mountain and into the privacy of his truck, Rafe thought about the woman he'd known briefly, but intimately, almost a decade ago. Colton Oil had mistakenly been excavating on government land. As the newly appointed CFO and eager to prove himself, Rafe had quickly and personally presented a financial offer to the government's attorney, Shelly Marston, to allow the company to continue drilling with more than fair remuneration to the government. He'd spared CO the cost of pulling out, applying for permission to drill and moving back in, and the government received more than usual compensation for the use of the land. And Shelly... She'd reminded him of Kerry. Same auburn hair. Same strength and sass. One night with her had told him that he couldn't go back. And that it was grossly unfair to another woman to use her as a stand-in.

Which was just as well. The next morning, when Shelly told him at breakfast that she'd appreciate it if, as part of their deal, he'd keep their night together just between the two of them, he'd noticed the wedding ring that had not been on her hand the day before.

She'd said that she and her husband were separated, going through some growing pains with careers that took them to different parts of the country, but that her night with Rafe had shown her how much she loved her family.

They'd used each other. Which had formed an odd bond between them. A completely nonsexual, noncommunicative bond. They'd go years without talking. But when either of them needed some professional advice in the area of the other's expertise, they picked up the phone trusting that it would be answered…

He saw a flash—a reflection off silver—a second before Kerry rounded the bend. Suddenly, they were forced cliffside, inches from going over.

His shoulder hit the door. He felt Kerry swerve again, felt the propulsion forward as his chest slammed into the seat belt, sensed a tightening within that braced for the unknown. And was aware of the thud as the Jeep came to a stop nose to nose with the mountain on the opposite side of the road. It took him a second to realize that flash of silver had been another vehicle.

By the time they'd stilled, his mind had caught up, was giving him instant replay in rapid staccato. And Kerry was saying, "Stay down," and was out of the vehicle, gun drawn, crouching with her door as a shield on one side and the mountain at her back.

Keeping his head below the windshield, Rafe slid across the seat, digging his thigh with the gearshift, and slid out her open door to crouch beside her.

"That was deliberate," she said. "He was waiting in this alcove for us to come around the corner."

"The ranger?" He'd eventually caught up to the situation. Knew that she'd had the wherewithal to swerve on the wrong side of the oncoming vehicle that had been clearly gunning to run them off the narrow road into the valley below.

She shrugged. "Who else?" The tension in her voice stung him. Alerting him anew to the danger of their situation.

"Something about us up there, looking into Tyler's death, sure had him paranoid," he said aloud, looking behind him, up what he could see of the part of the winding road they'd just descended. "We need to go," he said urgently, but softly, as though he could be overheard. "He's going to be coming back down."

She nodded. Did a three-sixty with her gun pointed out in front of her. And stopped.

"What's that?" she said, pointing with her gun to a space in front of her opened car door. With the falling dusk, he didn't immediately see what she was pointing at.

And then he did.

A boot. One that hadn't been there long enough even to get dusty or look unused. To have white bird droppings or chewed holes.

A boot that matched those the ranger had been wearing.

"Why would he leave without his boot?" Kerry asked. "If he was sitting there in his vehicle waiting for us, he wouldn't have been taking off his boots."

He knew she was right. Didn't want to worry about it at the moment. "Maybe he had an itch," he said, inanely, and then, "Come on, Kerry, we need to get down off this mountain before he comes back."

She nodded. *"I know."* And pushed the door forward enough that she could scoot around it, scraping against the mountain as she went, and then toward the boot.

Rafe followed her. He wasn't leaving her out there in the growing night alone.

"Look," she said, pointing toward tamped down underbrush. "Someone dragged something heavy..."

"Like a carton of ammunition."

She'd moved forward again, toward another drop-off on that side of the road. He'd grown up in those mountains, knew that they were filled with gullies and valleys, with steep slopes and dangerous, unforeseen drops. He knew how easy it would be for someone to fall and get hurt, if she missed just one step out there...

"Kerry, please," he said, heart pounding as he followed her.

"Or like a body," she said, her voice changed, shaking, and it took him a second to realize that she was responding to his comment about a carton of ammunition—or something else heavy having been dragged.

The land was mostly in shadows, but the setting sun still shone clearly in parts, highlighting the twisted body lying at an obviously lethal angle thirty feet below.

"Come on, we have to go," she said, swinging her gun from side to side, watching as they hurried back to the Jeep.

"That was the ranger." What the hell had they gotten themselves into? Not much point now in the phone call he'd been going to make—requesting a transfer for Grant Alvin. The ranger had just been sent much further away than he'd anticipated.

"I know it was. And I also know there's someone else out here. We have to go. To get help." She bit out the words with every step she took, pulling her phone off the clip at her hip. "There's no reception," she said, looking down, and in that instant, a shot fired out, dinged off the mountain less than a foot away from them.

Pushing Kerry into the Jeep in front of him, Rafe climbed in behind her, started the vehicle and sped off. Another shot rang out, but he made it round the bend before it could hit the car. He was driving too fast, prayed to God another vehicle wasn't coming up around a bend, but knew that he couldn't slow down. He had to get them the hell out of there before the gun behind them caught up.

What in the hell had just happened? Shaken mentally as well as physically, Kerry had a hand on the dash, turning in her seat to watch ahead of them as well as behind him, as Rafe sped the rest of the way down the mountain. Neither one of them spoke. All focus had to be on getting down to safety.

And when they'd reached the end of the drive, when Rafe had maneuvered them safely to the road leading into town, her brain started to shoot forward. The first thing she did was make a phone call, getting a specially trained rescue crew out to retrieve the ranger's body. While it was too dangerous to drive up the mountain in the dark, Chief Barco was positioning a car at the base of the mountain to prevent anyone from leaving before daybreak.

Of course, the perp could have already exited the drive, a minute or two after they did. With all of the turns in the road, she wouldn't have known if the black SUV she'd seen was right behind them or not. He could have waited until her Jeep was out of sight and then turned in the opposite direction. Away from town. He could be long gone.

Still, she'd intended to drop off Rafe and head back out there to explore at least the lower part of the mountain drive, but the chief had other ideas.

For the moment, she'd been ordered to stand down. Worse, he was sending a patrol car to sit outside her home for the rest of the night.

She'd been shot at. End of story.

Except that it wasn't.

"Who's out there?" she asked Rafe, completely frustrated as she hung up the phone. She wasn't good at inactivity. "And why?" Her whole life, the way she'd dealt with stress was by taking action. Same for combatting fear. You met it head-on. Dealt with it. You didn't hide in your home behind other officers at your front line.

"And what in the hell is going on up that mountain?" she asked when her first question received no answer.

"You asked him about guns and implied something about drugs," Rafe said slowly, his gaze focused on the road in front of them, as though he wasn't going to relax a muscle until they'd made the last five miles into town. "You really think that there's something big going on," he continued.

"Big enough to warrant killing Tyler," she said. "I know my brother wasn't involved in anything illegal that last year, but before that?" She hated that the question even had to be out there.

"It's possible he just stumbled into something," she continued, thinking out loud more than anything. "Tyler, I mean. But…you saw the photos from Tyler's fall," she said.

What she was about to say was the fact most on her mind at the moment. And the one she left out of her verbal report to the chief. Someone else might notice. They might not. For the moment, until she could think, she was keeping silent.

Rafe's nod was short. Succinct.

"Same way the head was bent back beneath the body…there's no way two falls could end up with the body landing so closely the same."

"Unless the bodies were held, probably by the neck, and then pushed in exactly the same way," Rafe said, earning her respect. He was right there with her.

Just as she'd have expected her best friend from long ago to be.

"I'm not getting why the ranger was killed," she said, less than a minute later. The town's lights were up ahead. Still another mile or so away. "He clearly wasn't out there protecting us. To the contrary, he wanted us gone. Like he was protecting something else."

She was back to the drugs and guns. She couldn't get off them, which told her that she was likely on the right path.

One that led, somehow, to Odin Rogers.

"Could be some kind of turf war and we drove into the middle of it."

"I need to get back up there and find the casings from the shots that were fired. To run ballistics on the guns."

Luckily they had a small crime lab right there in Mustang Valley, donated years ago by the Coltons.

"From what I heard of your conversation, you've been told to stay home for the rest of the night."

"That doesn't please me," she said. But she knew better than to disobey the chief's orders. He was chief for a reason. He knew the area. He knew his job. And she valued hers.

"I wonder if whoever killed the ranger was with him when he approached us? He had to get up there somehow and we never heard or saw another vehicle. Alvin walked up to us, walked away. Maybe whoever was driving the black SUV had parked the vehicle farther down and then followed the ranger up. Could be that person heard me asking Alvin about Tyler's death. But then he'd know that the guy was a jerk. Warned us off. Why would that get him killed?"

Rafe's shake of the head was brief. They'd entered Mustang Valley proper and he'd slowed to the speed limit.

"Whatever is going on must be big since it was worth killing not one, but two men over it."

She glanced at him. "You believe Tyler was murdered."

His quick glance thawed a small piece of her heart. "I trusted your instincts to begin with, but after this… it's clear you were right, Kerry. The problem is, how are we going to prove it?"

There was that "we" again.

The two of them. A team. Just as she'd once imagined they'd be.

But it was only for a moment.

Because, ultimately, nothing between them had changed. She couldn't trust him to have her back when life returned to normal and the Colton money and power became an issue again. Couldn't trust him to stick around.

And Kerry didn't like to think about the chances of her heart remaining intact if she gave it to him a second time and he crushed it in the dirt on his way out.

Chapter 5

The patrol car wasn't outside Kerry's house yet when Rafe pulled into her drive. Pushing the garage remote control, he parked in her garage, turned off the Jeep and handed her the keys. Then pushed the remote to close the garage door behind them, with his truck outside at the curb.

When those blue eyes of her turned on him, brows raised like she was questioning him, yet with a hint of their connection of old, he said, "I'm not leaving you here alone. I know, you're the trained cop with a gun and I'm just a numbers guy in expensive dress clothes, but two bodies, two sets of ears and eyes, are better than one."

"I wasn't going to argue with you sticking around for a bit," she told him, reaching for the door handle. "I was going to thank you."

She got out and led the way into the house, leaving him with his heart threatening to clog up his throat.

And then she offered him dinner. Leftover meat loaf, mashed potatoes and peas, a meal he'd have had as a young kid eating in the bunkhouse kitchen with his dad and the other cowboys, or a meal his dad might have prepared for him. Not anything he'd see on the Colton dinner table. Not unless it was hidden beneath garnishes and sauces that distinguished between cooking at home and having a chef. Or so he'd been told by Selina, Payne's second wife, who'd never made a secret of the fact that Rafe, as an adopted Colton, was merely a fly at her picnic.

Over the years, he'd grown accustomed to the wide variety of flavors, the combinations of spices that made eating a physical pleasure, rather than something one did to stay alive. He'd grown into those tastes. To seek them out, no matter the cost, when he traveled.

But to sit at Kerry's table with her—those leftovers were just fine. They'd taken their seats—his perpendicular to hers on two sides of her little four-seat table off to the right of her galley kitchen—when her doorbell rang. He hadn't been particularly worried about her safety at home in her neighborhood in the middle of town. Not many would try to kill a cop in front of other Mustang Valley citizens—who were known to watch each other's comings and goings—most particularly not in their little remote part of the Arizona desert. A lot of people carried guns for their own protection against whatever wildlife might venture into town looking for water. Most wouldn't hesitate to pull a weapon and use it to protect one of their own.

But when the bell rang, he was right behind her as she passed through the dining room to the living room and then the tiled area before the front door.

"I'm fine, Kay," she said, turning with a grin on her face that was quickly swept away.

He'd forgotten just how great he'd found the sound of his last name rolling off her lips as she jested with him. Said with just that same intonation.

Apparently she'd forgotten, for a second there at least, that he was a Colton now.

The knock came again, more urgently, and Kerry, with her hand at the gun she'd failed to remove when they'd returned home, looked through the peephole and then quickly opened the door.

"Lizzie, James," she said, stepping back to let the two blue uniformed officers into her home. "Don't tell me, the two of you are assigned to guard duty tonight?"

Lizzie shook her head. "James drew that straw," she said, with a wry glance at her partner.

"I volunteered for it," James corrected, his light red hair and the kind look in his hazel eyes giving the appearance of a man who could be a pushover. Rafe wasn't so sure he liked that this would be the guy in charge of Kerry's safety for the night until the man's gaze turned on him and he felt the full force of the steely stare.

"Aren't you one of the Coltons? Some kind of cousin to Spence?" the man asked. "You're the finance wizard, right?"

"Rafe," he said, holding out his hand, and feeling strangely self-conscious of his dust-covered expensive leather shoes as the man glanced down at his feet. "Kerry and I used to be friends, a long time ago," he heard himself explaining. And then wondering what in the hell had compelled him to answer a question this guy hadn't even asked.

"I knew her brother and when she told me that she thought maybe his death wasn't an accident, I wanted to hear more."

The man's look hadn't wavered from Rafe's face and it took him a second to realize that the other two law enforcement personnel in the room were standing there, watching the exchange.

"She's been saying that for a couple of years," the woman Kerry had called Lizzie said. With her long dark hair, back in a ponytail at the moment, and brown eyes, she was quite pretty, even in uniform. He hoped she was stronger than she looked. "Why you just taking an interest now?" Her gaze locked on his, as well.

Kerry could jump in anytime. Save his ass. Give whatever explanation she wanted them to have.

Or he'd give his own…

"We just reconnected, since Payne's shooting," he said. "I had no idea Tyler's death wasn't an accident."

"Until tonight, it was," the man, James, said.

And then Lizzie piped in, "The case was closed, but now, who knows?" She shrugged. "With two bodies found dead in kind of the same manner, someone might have some questions." When she turned to Kerry, Rafe felt like he might be off whatever hook they'd impaled him on, at least for the moment.

He listened intently as Lizzie told Kerry, "The chief and I headed straight up there as soon as you called it in. The rescue crew is still in the gully, getting the ranger out, but we went up the drive and couldn't find anything, Kerry. No shell casings. No sign of anyone around. Just a broken agave arm and the boot you saw. Again, it looks like he could have jumped. But there's a little bit stronger evidence at this point that he might have been pushed. With that boot there. We're looking for fingerprints but don't expect to get anything."

"The boot obviously came off while he was being dragged," Kerry said. "He'd have been digging his foot into the ground, trying to get a hold, to stop himself from going over, but whoever dragged him was a helluva lot stronger than he was and dragged him right out of his boot."

"That's what it looks like." Lizzie's attention was only on Kerry at that point. As if the women were friends who spoke their own language in between the words they said. The type who understood the nuances and emotions not being expressed.

"The heel of the boot was caught on a root."

So Kerry's hunch had been right.

Again. He wasn't surprised. She'd always impressed him with her intuitive observations. Even as a kid.

"We'll be going back up in the morning," Lizzie continued. "Maybe when it's light, we'll see more, but for now the only thing we have is the wider tire tracks of the SUV, just as you described. We drove all the way up the hill, by the way. There was no sign of the vehicle up there, so either the guy has a hiding place where he parks it up there someplace…"

"Or he's long gone," Kerry finished for her. "Someone shot at us as we were leaving, which means someone was close by. He could easily have just followed us down the hill and took off as we came back to town."

He'd already entertained the same uneasy thought. His family's ranch was on the opposite side of town, but still out there. He didn't like knowing there were ranch hands with families in little cabins with a crazy killer free.

"Which is why I'm going to be right outside until dawn, and people are up and about and it's less likely that someone would get into town undetected," James said.

"And I need to get back to the station," Lizzie said, and then both officers looked at Rafe, as if Rafe had just been given his cue to leave.

"I'm going to hang around here," he said, without looking at Kerry. Her friends were right there. If she wanted him out of there, he'd be gone in an instant.

"We were just sitting down to dinner," she told the two in uniform. And then asked James, "Have you had something to eat?"

"I've got a cooler full out in the car," he told her. "And a pee bottle, too."

Rafe could have done without that piece of information.

But then the two were gone, leaving him and Kerry all alone in the watched cocoon that was her house. The awareness of what had just happened—the two of them acknowledging, in front of others, that they wanted to spend more time together that evening— simmered between them and they just stood there, on that small area of tile, looking at each other.

Kerry broke the eye contact first, heading back

through the dining area and kitchen to the food gone cold. She sat anyway, as though eating a cold dinner didn't faze her at all.

"James might look like an easygoing nice guy," she said, scooping up mashed potatoes and then meat on the same bite. "And he is nice. He's perfectly compliant on any occasion that warrants it, but he's as tough as they come when he perceives a wrongdoing. Or a threat to any townspeople."

He nodded, not sure if she was reassuring him as to their safety, or warning him in regard to hers. Should he try to make a move on her.

Despite needing her to know that as much as he longed to grab his Kerry into his arms and never let her go, he had no intention of touching her. Not when even a chaste kiss in the past had been red-hot. So he sat. Forked cold food. And ate it.

While they ate, Rafe loosened his tie, talked about all the exotic foods he'd eaten, most of which he'd enjoyed. If he'd set out to remind Kerry of the vast differences between them, he needn't have bothered. His being a Colton was something she was never, ever going to forget.

And while he did the dishes he insisted on taking care of, she went to the restroom. She'd been holding it for a while, and hadn't wanted to go with him in the house. Seemed way too…personal, too intimate, for what she needed him to be. Everyone peed. She just didn't want to go do it with him there.

"You should call the hospital, check on your father," she told him as she came back down the hall and found him standing in the dining room, glancing at her wall. She'd deliberately used the parental designation rather than Payne's name.

"I just did," he told her. "No change."

She wondered who he talked to... Ace? Another sibling? Payne's third wife, Genevieve? The spouse was always the first suspect when someone was shot, but both Genevieve and Payne's second wife, Selina Barnes Colton, had airtight alibis: security footage from the RRR during the time of the shooting. Genevieve in the mansion, Selina walking from her car to her smaller house on the property, carrying in bags of shopping from someplace farther than Mustang Valley, based on the bags' logos.

Weird that Selina would have gone shopping while the rest of the family dealt with the shock of Ace Colton's surprise heritage, the knowledge that the eldest heir had been switched at birth and subsequently been stripped of his position as CEO of Colton Oil...

Her mental switch to her current case was a coping mechanism, she knew. Recognized it. Anytime things started to rattle her emotional ground, she focused on a case. Made her great at her job. And still single at thirty-six.

"I made another call, too," Rafe said, still facing the wall plastered with the last ten years of Tyler's life. "To a government attorney who works with the Forest Service. I asked for a fast track on any warrant or request that may come through for Grant Alvin's employment record, or for anything else pertaining to anyone working that mountain."

To show her how powerful he was? To push his weight around?

He turned and her gaze hooked up with the depth of emotion in those so-familiar blue eyes of his. He'd called because he cared.

Because he was committed to helping her find out what had happened to Tyler. She got the message. He was going to help and then he'd be going back to his real life—the one where he could pick up the phone and call a US attorney after eight o'clock at night.

She made a note of that, too.

"I had no idea it was going to be so hard, seeing you again." The longing in his words, barely above a whisper, shot through her with the force of a blast.

She couldn't go down that road again. "It's a little weird, yeah, but fine, too," she said, arranging folders on the table.

"I used to watch you." He'd put his hands in his pockets and was standing there not bothering to hide the glistening in his eyes. "After you'd get home from school, you'd get on Annabelle and ride out to our hill. Every day, when you'd disappear out of sight, I'd pretend I was out there with you…"

"Don't, Rafe." He'd watched her? It could be creepy. But it was Rafe. Needing her.

Just as she'd needed him.

Even in their separation they'd been together? The idea soothed her.

And nothing had changed.

"I'd sit up in my room and picture you out there with someone else. Someone who would love you as much as I did, and not leave you…"

Picturing the thirteen-year-old man-child he'd been, all alone in his room at the mansion—she even knew which window to picture since she'd looked up to it often enough over the years—she didn't want to care.

He'd made his choice. But…

"Payne Colton's a powerful man." She gave him what little leeway she'd been able to find for him over the years. For the young Rafe, that was. "You were a kid with no other family. It would have been suicide to challenge him over a girl at that age," she said.

He swallowed so hard she noticed his Adam's apple bobbing.

And she thought of the eighteen years after he'd no longer been a kid and still hadn't even bothered to call. To send her a card. To acknowledge she existed.

"You were right to stay away," she said then. Because clarity was a wonderful thing when it came loaded in truth. And a total bitch, too, with the pain it brought. "It would have hurt too badly to be in touch with our lives so completely different."

They might inhabit the same twenty-mile radius of the universe, but their worlds were so distant they'd done so without ever running into each other. Stone-cold truth.

"Tonight…when that shot rang out…when I thought at first that you'd been shot…" She looked at him. She should never have looked at him. "You're in my heart, Kerry. You're there. Exactly where you've always been. As much as you've always been. I just need you to know that."

For a brief second, her spirit soared. She was young again. With a heart filled with hope and possibility.

With plans. With a heart that knew how to dream. And then reality hit. Him standing there in his expensive clothes, in front of a wall filled with her brother's murder details.

She wasn't the only one who'd been hurt by Rafe's defection. And he hadn't said a word about coming back, either. About being friends in the future.

Because he couldn't. She got that. He'd been a Colton for too long. His family depended on him, and he on them, too, she figured: whether he liked that or not.

She wanted to tell him that he was in her heart, too, but that door wasn't open. Not even a little bit. Her secrets had been shut away for so long, she wasn't even sure what was in there anymore.

Didn't really want to know.

"When I got back from college, I moved out of the mansion," he told her. "I built a house…"

"You don't live in the mansion?"

But that's where she'd been picturing him. In the present. But in the past, too. All those years, every time she'd driven out that way, she'd always looked out in the distance and pictured him up on the third floor, in a corner room separate from his other siblings. He'd used to describe the place to her: all the bathrooms, the carpeting so thick you don't hear steps when you walk…

"I built my own place…" he was saying again, and she stopped him.

"*Had* it built, you mean."

He wasn't in the mansion. She had no idea where

he lived. Couldn't picture his home, but it shouldn't matter.

She just didn't like that kind of surprise. Some things were meant to stay neatly in their place.

"I hired help, yes, but I did as much of the work myself as I could," he told her, surprising her. "It took me over a year." He stood there, meeting her gaze, holding on to her with it, like he needed her to see inside him.

She wasn't going to look. Didn't he get that? He'd taken away that right, once. She wasn't going to let him take it from her again.

And couldn't live with it and not live with him.

"I built it on our land, Kerry. Our spot on the other side of the hill behind the barn."

No. He. Did. Not.

He was living on the one acre in the world that was sacred to her? The one that had sustained her during her years with him, allowing them to be friends unseen, and the ones after him, too. The one place in the world where she'd always been able to find solace?

She'd cried more tears in that dust and dirt than she'd cried since. Ever.

Not at her father's funeral. And not at Tyler's, either.

She'd cried more for Rafe than for either of the men who were family to her.

And she couldn't do this. She wasn't that girl anymore. He'd killed her.

"You broke my heart, Rafe."

Chapter 6

Rafe might have killed the girl she'd been, but she wasn't a girl anymore. She was a grown woman with a life that satisfied her. She could risk her life saving others because she didn't have anyone who was counting on her, anyone who'd be devastated, if she was killed.

Not that there was usually all that much danger in Mustang Valley. Lately, though… First with the murder of a bodyguard hired to protect the president of Robertson Renewable Energy Corporation, Bowie Robertson. Then attempts made on the lives of Bowie and Rafe's sister Marlowe, and then Payne Colton's shooting, and now a ranger killed and someone shooting at her and Rafe…

"How come you never married?" Kerry plopped down to one of the six chairs tucked into her dining room table—an antique she'd restored. After everything that had happened in the past few hours, she needed a moment to regroup. To be the woman she was, not the young girl she'd once been.

She needed to see Rafe Colton as the man he was now, not the boy he'd been.

He sat, too, leaving a chair between them. "Never found a woman I wanted to live with for the rest of my life. How about you?"

She'd brought that on, she supposed. *Don't ask if you don't want to be asked.* Being a detective, one who spent her days asking questions of others with it understood that her own thoughts didn't come to play in the interaction, she'd maybe become a little rusty at the personal stuff.

"I'm not all that fond of men," she said. "I just don't believe they're wired to be what I need in a relationship."

She saw the verbal bullet hit him. Hurt for him. And couldn't lie about what his choices had done to her. Not just his, of course. Her father—he'd tried his best but most definitely had not been a man she could rely on, other than to be able to trust that if he wasn't drunk, he would be soon.

And Tyler—he'd fallen down that same rabbit hole.

"Then you haven't known the right men," Rafe finally said.

She shrugged. *Maybe.*

"There are a lot of happily married women in the world. And men who've risked everything for their families. For their country. For…"

Holding up a hand, Kerry smiled. "I get it," she said. "I actually work with several of them."

And at home, she had trust issues.

"I've found that my life is happier, I'm more at peace inside, when I have no expectations where men are concerned," she said, giving him more than she'd ever admitted aloud.

Because he was Rafe?

She hoped not. She wanted to believe that she was just a bit more open—a smidge vulnerable—because they'd just been shot at and she had a cop stationed outside her door.

"What about kids?" His question hit a very sore spot.

"I always wanted them." She was only confirming what he already knew. She wanted four so that they'd always have each other, but no more than that, so there would be at least one parental hand per kid at all times. At thirteen, the theory had sounded valid.

Fooling with a corner of the folder in front of her, a compilation of information about the women her brother had hooked up with over the years, she said, "Now... I'm thirty-six. I'd have to meet a guy, fall in love and get pregnant in pretty quick order..."

She'd been feeling the pressure since her thirtieth birthday. The idea that time was running out. More now, she was starting to settle for a new reality. One where she didn't have kids of her own. But she had a career she truly loved. Friends she truly loved. A town filled with people who looked out for her. A home that welcomed her every time she walked in the door.

"I'm just so damned sorry, Kerry."

Rafe's words hit too deep. She shook her head. "Don't be," she said. "I made my choices just like you made yours." And one of them had been not to settle for less than she'd felt for Rafe. She'd rather live alone than be with a man she always felt was second-best.

"I guess I should get going." He stood up. She walked with him toward her front door.

"I don't like the idea of you driving back out to the ranch," she said, suddenly not complacent, or content, at all. "Whoever shot at us likely knows who you are. He could know that your truck was parked out in front of my house. Might be waiting for you to be alone."

"I'm not running scared," he told her. "And I'm not stupid, either. I can tell if I'm being followed. I have a rifle in the truck. And I'm an excellent shot."

He'd been a decent shot when she'd known him. She'd been better. They'd target practiced with BB guns a lot. She concentrated on the target. He'd always been looking at her.

"Still…maybe it would be better if you wait until daylight to head out that far…"

She had a cop at her door. Surely it wasn't paranoia to think driving ten miles out in the desert could be dangerous.

He'd stopped in the foyer. Turned. Was a foot away and staring her right in the eye. "Are you asking me to spend the night here?"

No. No! She'd been afraid for his safety. Remembered the drive back into town that night. How thankful she'd been to see the lights of town. Hadn't wanted him back on any ten-mile stretch alone in the dark until they knew more.

Right?

She didn't expect him to hang with her all night.

Didn't want him to.

Not really. The woman she was knew better.

"I'm sure the Dales Inn has a room," she said. January was one of the biggest tourist months in Arizona, but Mustang Valley wasn't a hot spot.

He nodded and turned back toward the door.

Disappointment flooded her. Hers? His? She'd always hated to let him down. Had done everything she could not to make that happen. Especially after he'd been adopted and told her how lonely he was, living in that big mansion with a new father who didn't seem to put a whole lot of stock in having him around. He used to say that her friendship was the most important thing in his life.

Had that been a lie?

Or had it just changed?

Did it matter?

"Good night, then."

He reached for the door handle.

"Rafe."

"Yeah?" he asked, turning again.

"You'll stay in town, right?"

He studied her, frowning. "It really means that much to you?"

With a nod she looked up at him. "It really does."

"Then yes, I'll stay in town, rather than returning to the ranch."

Good. Phew.

"I'll call you in the morning," he said.

She nodded. Couldn't stop looking at him. Remembering the shots firing, needing to know that he was okay. Far more than she'd cared if she was.

Taking a step closer just happened. He seemed to get that. Leaned down just enough... And their lips touched.

Tentatively. Softly. Like two kids raging with hormones, budding with love and filled with curiosity. Two kids who didn't have any idea what they were doing.

But instead of being ripped apart by angry words from Payne Colton, who'd followed them because Rafe had unknowingly taken a horse that Payne hadn't wanted ridden, they continued to kiss.

Rafe's lips opened, seeming hungry with desire. They moved against hers, strongly, confidently, eliciting a response from her she hadn't known she was capable of giving. Her tongue moved of its own accord, meeting his, exploring. She sucked at his lips. Pressed hard, needing it all to be real. His arms were around her, flattening her against him, and she held on to his head. His neck. Pulling him to her.

They turned, and she fell back against the door, his body against hers, holding her there. Molding her. She could hardly breathe. Couldn't think.

Didn't want to stop.

Ever.

"I'm..." Gasping, Rafe didn't finish his sentence.

She put a shaking finger to his lips. "Don't apologize," she whispered. Begged, more like it.

Yeah, she was "only the help," but she needed to be good enough to be worthy of his kiss. Like any other woman he'd known.

"I wasn't going to apologize," he told her, one hand against the door just above her head. He leaned over her, still breathing hard. "I was going to tell you that I'm in over my head."

His blue eyes were shadowed with passion, but surprisingly clear, too. Honest.

She had to be the woman she was, she reminded herself, not even sure in the moment what those words meant.

"We're both adults." She tried to swallow, to ease the dryness in her throat. Pretty much whispered, "We don't have to make this more difficult than it is."

His gaze intensified. She could feel her chin starting to tremble as she stared up at him. "We just have unfinished business." She said what she needed to believe was true. "Something that just needs finishing." *Just. Just. Just.*

"Just" put limitations on it.

She was sure it did. That she was facing reality. Had her eyes wide-open.

"I've had the hots for you since I was twelve," she told him, hiding under her detective guise, the cover that slid down over her emotions when she was dealing with a potentially heartbreaking case. Like many first responders, she knew how to find her calm. Her strength. Knew how to brace against pain that was too unimaginable to bear. "It's natural for someone to be left in this state after feeling what we felt at such an impressionable age, and having had it ripped away as we did, without allowing it to run its course and fade naturally." She'd been working on the situation, the feelings for Rafe that just wouldn't fade, for years.

"It's also natural to romanticize something we lost. To grieve for it." Counseling she'd sought after a reckless stint of meaningless lovers in college had taught her that. "Which then tends to strengthen those remembered feelings. Make them more than they are."

If she just kept talking, his hard-on might fade. Maybe they could still defuse this enough to get him out the door and her into a cold shower.

"You're proposing that we have sex and get it out of our systems?"

Of course she wasn't. Was she? There was merit in the theory…

"You have a better plan?" she asked him. "We live too close to think that, now that the smoldering spark has been lit, we won't both be burned by it if we don't put it out."

"And you think a one-night fling will do that."

She had no idea what she thought. She only knew that there was no hope of a future for them. Not just because of his choices, but because she wasn't ever going to be able to trust him not to turn his back on her, to ditch her, to stab her back if one of the Coltons insisted he do so. Maybe he'd stand up to Payne this time. Maybe not.

But the heart didn't forget when someone chose one person over another. Not when the one *not* chosen was so irreparably damaged by that choice.

"I think it's our only hope at this point." The truth came to her. Loud and clear. She had to get this man out of her system or spend the rest of her life grieving for him.

She needed a strong dose of the real Rafe Colton to

replace the romanticized version of the man her fantasies had created within her.

The strength of his desire, pressing against her, grew stronger. More insistent.

"But it would just have to be the one night, Rafe. Whether it gets rid of the attraction or not. I'm not that young girl anymore. I don't even want to be. And I won't be in a relationship that can't lead to marriage."

He blinked, his lids staying closed a second or two too long, and then he nodded. "I wish it could be different."

She didn't. Not anymore.

But she pulled his lips down to hers with a hunger that was never going to be satisfied.

Not in one night.

Not ever.

Chapter 7

He wasn't going to have sex with Kerry Wilder. She deserved more than a one-night stand. And he'd lost his rights to her long ago.

But when she planted her lips on his, there was no way in hell or on earth that Rafe could reject her.

Kerry's lips weren't the tentative soft touch he remembered, and yet their combination of softness and strength, hesitance and confidence, drove him to devour them. To mate his tongue with hers like he needed to mate their bodies. Entering her, moving in her. Knowing her.

He kissed her hard. And he kissed her soft. His hand still pressed up against the door, and then, turning again so that she was in his arms, he was against the door. Leaning. Taking her weight and his. Pulling her weight against him until he could feel every inch of her body with every inch of his.

The softness of her breasts pressed against him was heaven, and sheer torture. There was nothing small or dainty about them, and yet they were vulnerable. Just like her. Needing gentle love.

She went for his shirt, loosening his tie more, first, and because it hurt too much to think of being done yet, he let her. Nothing dangerous in baring *his* chest.

Those smaller, warm fingers moving on him were a shock, created a pleasure so intense he almost cried out. How could Kerry's blunt-nailed fingers be so much more powerful on his skin than anything else that had ever touched him?

With her lips still plastered to his she slid her fingers through the hair on his chest, raising goose bumps there—and raising his nipples, too. Her tongue seemed to speak to him in rhythm with those fingertips and he forgot to think.

"God, you feel so good," he gasped as he took a breath and then ravished her lips some more. He'd never been much of a kissing man. Couldn't make sense of the effect her kisses were having on him.

His hands were plastered on her back. He wasn't consciously keeping them there, but somewhere, something in him knew that he couldn't move them.

Because they'd both fall?

Because he couldn't let go?

Because if he did they'd get him into trouble?

It all became moot when she reached behind herself and grabbed his hand. He liked that too, holding hands with her while they kissed. And then, before he knew her intent, she'd laid his hand down. Let it go.

Centered on her breast.

He broke their kiss, words choking him. The sound came out no more than a groan, a pained one filled with an ecstasy that was shocking him.

He couldn't let go of her breast. Couldn't disappoint her. So he held it. Memorizing the contours. Knowing the sensation would always be a part of him.

Her nipples were hard and he wanted to pleasure her, to make the kiss one she'd remember for the rest of her life.

With fondness.

He needed it to matter to her.

And so he allowed his hand to move on her. His fingers found a nipple through her oxford shirt and what had to be an unlined bra covering her. He teased with the expertise he'd gained over his years as a man, grown from the boy who'd had to leave her.

His knowledge of the female body led him to her other breast—not wanting to leave her only half-cared-about. And then, as she moaned and moved within his fingers, he found the buttons on her shirt, had them undone, and her bra, too, in just a few quick seconds. Just so that he could give her the utmost pleasure.

Maybe something was driving him to give her the best she'd ever had of what little he could share with her. Thoughts weren't real clear.

They became even less so when her hand cupped the hard-on that had crept up toward his belly button, the head of which was bulging uncomfortably against his belt buckle. Which was why he let her loosen the buckle. Just to give him some relief while they stood there.

When, minutes later, she went for his fly, too, he had no reason to allow himself the relief, other than not wanting to deny her anything she wanted.

They moved over to her couch, leaving their clothes in a trail on the floor between him and the door, his hands shaking as he pulled a condom out of his wallet and watched as she slid it home, before he realized that he'd missed the key point.

He'd been right.

He wasn't going to have sex with Kerry.

They were going to make love.

The moment she spread her legs and felt Rafe slide inside her, Kerry changed. Irrevocably. She moved with him, let herself fly away to a place where only physical pleasure, sensation, existed. Pulsed against him with a mind-blowing orgasm as his release poured out, and it was all different. She was different.

As he collapsed against her, she held him willingly, with no thought to getting the weight off her. Getting up. Cleaning up. She was his home for as long as he needed to lie there.

And he was her protection from a lifetime of aloneness: for as long as these moments could last.

She knew they would end. But she also knew she'd never regret what had happened. Her entire life she'd been on hold, waiting for something.

And she'd just had it.

She didn't know how she knew. Wasn't sure where

it all led her, but she knew that she was finally free of the not knowing. She didn't have to wonder anymore.

She just had to figure out how to live without it.

But not yet.

"Please stay," she said. And then, afraid that he'd think she was begging, asking for more than would ever be there, she said. "Just for tonight. Just until dawn and you can see more clearly to drive out to the ranch."

His nod made her happy.

Kerry called James before she took Rafe back to her bedroom. She let her fellow officer know that she'd talked Rafe into staying with her, for his own protection, and that he'd said her couch was plenty comfortable.

Which he had, when they'd first lain down naked and she'd mentioned that she had a perfectly good bed with sheets.

Neither of them had been willing to hold on until they could get there.

"You're always thinking, Kerry Wilder," Rafe said, grinning as he picked her up and carried her down the only hallway in the place. He had a few doors to choose from: a bathroom, a spare bedroom she used as a catchall and an office, and her bedroom suite. She let him figure it out.

And didn't bother pointing out the light switch when they entered her room. She was not taking any chances on James witnessing the shadow of a wealthy Colton carrying her to bed.

Their relationship had been secret since they were five years old—because no one understood.

Because they had to guard against others' opinions. Warnings. Demands.

He settled her against the comforter and she pulled it down as she scooted her naked butt underneath it, stopping only when she felt the sheet beneath her. When he asked for the bathroom, she pointed to the left of the closet door, and while he was gone, flipped on her bedside lamp. In case James was watching to see that she made it back to her room.

By the time Rafe had flushed, run water and turned it off, she figured she was safe to turn off the light, and did so.

The rest of the night would be theirs.

Their lifetime. Their secret.

Their little piece of happiness.

She didn't sleep much. That night they'd made love again. Talked softly about food and movies and sports teams. Changes in the world that made it more inclusive—and scarier, too, as guns entered schools and churches. They held each other through it all, agreed on a lot of it. And they talked about their early days, times on the ranch when his birth father had been alive. And then when only hers had.

They talked about family. About love. About things that hurt.

But discussion of the breakup and the years apart was nowhere to be found in their few hours of seclusion. After a third coming together in body as well as spirit, after she rode him hard, almost as though she could somehow get him out of her system, figuring, as he bucked into her that he was getting her out of his. She slid off him, lying close but not touching, and pretended to sleep.

Letting him get some sleep.

She tried. She meant to. A full day of police work waited ahead. But for those last few hours, she was purely and completely selfish. Taking care of herself.

She lay there with a grown-up Rafe Kay in her bed. Listened to him breathe. Memorized the rhythm. Inhaled his earthy, postlovemaking scent, watched the rise and fall of his chest. Got as close to his warmth in her bed as she could without actually touching him.

For those hours she allowed herself to love him. She dozed on and off, wanting to sleep with him beside her, and before dawn arrived, she said goodbye.

It had to happen.

As wonderful as the night had been, it was just a figment of the past's imagination. She had been waiting all their lives for this to happen. And now that it had, now that they'd had a chance to say an actual goodbye, they could finally both move on.

Rafe was up and dressed when Kerry woke from her last doze. After she'd said a mental goodbye and let him go.

"I'll go make some coffee," he said, seeing her sit up. He wasn't looking her in the eye, and she understood. Appreciated the distance that was going to make the morning after easier.

The pain she felt, the grief, was not new to her. But she was better equipped to deal with it at thirty-six than she'd been at thirteen.

Deciding to shower and dress for work before she joined him, she half expected him to be gone when she got out to the living room. When he wasn't, she peeked outside. The sun was barely rising, and James was still sitting upright in his police car, glancing at his phone, and then around him, in the rearview mirror and back to his phone.

In her light brown pants, white shirt and loafers, with her gun already strapped at her waist, and her long, still-wet hair back in a ponytail, she called the officer and let him know she was up and he was good to go.

And turned to find Rafe standing there, looking all elite and important even in second-day clothes, handing her a cup of coffee that wasn't black. She took a sip. And wondered why he'd bothered to make such a clean knot in his tie when he'd just be going home to shower and change.

"You had hazelnut creamer in the fridge, so I figured that's how you like it," he said. She did, sometimes.

"I was wrong," he said, when she took a second sip.

She shouldn't have been surprised that he'd known. Her expression had given him more than her mouth and brain intended him to have.

"I need a couple of cups of straight black first thing in the morning," she admitted. "The creamer was left over from a Christmas party, but I do use it sometimes when I'm working late from home."

He had a cup in hand. She couldn't see how he took his.

It seemed fitting to her—the fact that they didn't

know such a simple thing about each other. It was telling. Put things in perspective.

"So what happens next?" he asked her, his gaze too intent for her to pretend the question was anything but personal.

"I had a text from Al… Chief Barco. We're going to talk this morning to discuss an investigation into Odin Rogers." Finally. At least something good had come out of the harrowing night they'd had—and a ranger losing his life. Her peers were finally ready to acknowledge that there might be something in her hunch that her brother's death hadn't been accidental. And the chief was willing to listen to her other hunches on the subject.

"I've done a lot of investigation already," she said, nodding toward the wall that was partially visible from where they stood in the living room. "The chief and Dane, Detective Dane Howman, are coming over this morning to go over what I've got. And I have to focus on finding out who shot Payne," she reminded him— specifically in that moment the reminder was personal. And intended for both of them.

And to that end, she'd spent her time in the shower, after shedding a few very private tears, focusing her mind on her current assignment. "Who's going to run Colton Oil now that Ace is out as CEO and Payne is in a coma?"

"The board already voted to have Marlowe take over as CEO." He'd know, being a member of that board.

Marlowe was the fourth-oldest Colton sibling. She'd been the talk of the station recently, as PJ worked to catch her stalker. From what Kerry had gathered at the hospital the other night when she'd gone into the waiting room to bring Ace Colton in for questioning, Marlowe was pregnant and had just announced her engagement to rival energy executive Bowie Robertson.

Grayson Colton, a first responder, wasn't on the board, nor was Asher, but Ainsley, Marlowe's older sister was.

Maybe Marlowe knew that, with Payne also out of commission, she'd be next in command, and, with perhaps some pushing from her lover who just happened to be the son of the owner of Colton Oil's biggest rival, a company that lobbied for green energy, had decided to have Payne taken out.

Recent attempts had been made on her own life. That changed a person. Could have made her temporarily aggressive.

"Is it possible Marlowe's involved in the shooting?" she asked Rafe. It was a question she'd ask other members of the board, as well. She was working a case. Living real life.

Setting down his coffee cup with a bit of force— he took it black, she noted—he asked, "Do you really think all of the Coltons are that heartless?"

She'd hurt him. Or angered him. "I honestly don't know…"

She'd talked to Marlowe at the hospital. Hadn't had a sense that she was capable of violence. To the contrary, she'd seemed to be one of the calming factors in the room. Logical. Still, she had to be aware of possible motive…

The sound of glass shattering broke into her consciousness just seconds before a heavy object sailed by her peripheral vision and landed on the floor just behind her.

Aware of her front window in shatters, and of Rafe moving toward her, Kerry focused on the object. A large brick.

With a note rubber-banded around it.

MIND YOUR OWN BUSINESS DETECTIVE OR RICHIE RICH IS NEXT.

Chapter 8

Rafe was right behind Kerry as she raced out the front door. He didn't have a gun in his hand, as she did, but he had a sharp eye. The street was quiet. Serene.

He didn't say a word as he looked around one corner of the house, following her example as she'd looked around the other. He peered under some flowering bushes that lined the front of her home. Walked to the sidewalk out front. Didn't find so much as a footprint.

And neither did she, as she told him after she'd checked both neighboring yards and her own backyard in case the culprit was hiding close by.

She was already on the phone to the station by the time they headed back inside, and Rafe heard her say she'd write up the report and log the brick as evidence before sending it to forensics.

If he didn't know her, he'd assume she was 100 percent on the job, focused and unaffected by having just had the front of her house shattered, leaving a gaping hole that made her living room open to the outside elements.

She was focused, but she wasn't unaffected. He saw the unease in the way the blue of her eyes deepened.

Her next call was to someone who agreed to come out within the hour to get the front window boarded up.

"He thinks he can have a new window in later today," she told Rafe as she hung up from the call. He had calls to make as well, but needed to make sure she was okay, first.

Cop or no, she lived alone and had just been vandalized.

Whether or not seeing her was forbidden to him, he couldn't keep pretending he didn't care for her. The way his heart was pounding at the thought that she could have been hurt—not because he could have been— was right there in his face. Kerry was…special.

And not just because they'd had sex. Spent the night in each other's arms. He'd done that with other women.

None of them made him feel the way she did.

He wasn't just walking away.

"It's a standard size for houses around here, so he has one in stock," she added, putting her phone down on the dining room table and opening one of the files on Odin Rogers.

His cue to go.

He read it clearly.

"I'm going home to shower, but then I'll be back in

town," he told her. "To see Payne, and with all that's been going on, I've got some work to catch up on at the office." The oil was drilled, bought and sold whether the boss was lying in a coma or sitting at his desk. "But I'm volunteering to help you on this, Kerry. Whatever you need…even if it's just an ear to run things by as you think it all through…"

He was referring to her brother, but would do anything he could to help figure out who wanted Payne dead, too. Any of the family would.

"You are not helping me anymore," she said, her tone tense as she swung around to face him. "I never should have taken you up there to begin with. Now you're a target, too, and I'll never forgive myself if something happens to you because I put you in danger. You and your family already have enough to deal with."

The force with which she spewed her words moved him so much it took a few seconds to respond. Regardless of circumstances between them, she cared.

But then, the passion in her lovemaking the night before had already given him that much.

They both cared. And it wasn't enough.

The sad story of their lives.

"I was compared to a cartoon character. Richie Rich," he said with a shrug and a poor attempt at a grin. "But I already planned on hiring a private security detail…"

"Right, because the Coltons have the funds to do such things. I should have already thought of that. I'm glad."

He saw her swallow heavily between her first and

second sentence and noted the brief lack of professionalism in the way she gestured wildly with her hands,
as well as the hint of bitterness that came and went
from her expression.

He chose to pass them by.

"So you'll let me help?"

"No." She turned back to the table filled with details
of her investigation. "Whoever killed my brother, and
the ranger, is worried about what I might know. And,
now you, too, clearly. The deeper I delve, the more
worried he's going to get."

"Can't get any worse for me than it already is," he
told her, walking around to face her across the table.
"He won't have any way of knowing whether you update me or not. Or whether or not I'm going to hire a
private detective to see what he can sniff out. I'm already in, Kerry."

Her glance wasn't as discouraging as it had been.
He got that she didn't want him in danger. He got even
more that, after the night they'd spent, she had to push
him away. Hard.

He didn't get why he couldn't just step back and
let it happen.

But he knew for certain that he was in as deep as
it got.

And staying in.

At least until they caught her brother's killer.

After Rafe left, Kerry mentally reviewed the evidence. Three days after Payne Colton got shot, a ranger
was killed and her life was threatened. These three
felonies—along with the murder of Bowie Robert-

son's bodyguard and the attempted murders of Robertson and Rafe's sister—were more crimes than their little town with its few officers and detectives usually saw in a year. And that didn't include the attempts on Bowie Robertson's life over the previous weeks.

She'd been looking into Tyler's death for the whole two years, but the day that Rafe Colton got involved, someone died and she and Rafe were targeted.

And that came right after an attempt on his adoptive father's life.

Was she losing perspective by thinking that the two incidents could be related?

Tyler had grown up on Payne's property. Was the killer someone who either worked for Colton Oil or Rattlesnake Ridge Ranch? Was Payne's shooter the same person? Someone Tyler might have known as "Big B"?

She didn't think so. The attempt on Payne's life had come right after the family had made the shocking discovery that Ace Colton had been switched at birth. That he wasn't a Colton at all. Right after he'd been fired as CEO of the family's multibillion-dollar company.

The kind of trouble Tyler had been in was nowhere near the same league.

And the danger she and Rafe were in wasn't, either.

Which was why she didn't answer his call later that morning, only listening to his voice mail because it could have something to do with his father's case.

His father. Maybe if she thought of Payne that way often enough, her adjustment to the present would be easier.

He'd just been calling to check in. Asked her to call him back.

She didn't.

Instead she did her job, going with Dane to have a talk with Odin Rogers at his residence. The vest and pocket watch might have looked good on the supposed drug dealer if his paunch didn't strain buttons and the chain of the watch wasn't stretched to capacity across his girth. The man really should be in the hair gel business, given how much slime he had pasting long strands of what hair he had left over bald patches. When they asked him about any business he might have in the mountains, if he was ever up Mustang Mountain Drive, asked him about people he knew, he was as innocently ignorant as always to their faces. So she asked him about sources for his wealth. He hadn't had a job in the valley for as long as she could remember.

He claimed to be independently wealthy from investments he'd made with an inheritance he'd received from a life insurance policy when his father died.

Right. If life insurance came in the guise of inherited contracts in the illegal weapons trade or drug business. As close to the southern border as they were, such goings-on were not merely suspicions, but a known way of life.

Catching them, proving things, was another story. Just when they'd think they were onto something a deal would be made to catch a bigger fish. But not this time.

Kerry wasn't into fishing for size. She wanted the man stopped and brought to justice.

She and Dane were just leaving the man on his porch when Kerry noticed a pair of boots sitting under a bench by the door. Not freshly shined fancy ones like Odin was currently wearing, but a used pair with the same worn-down heel on the right boot as the pair he currently wore. Because Odin walked with a slight limp.

It wasn't the slight tilt to the heel that interested her, however. It was the cactus needle sticking out slightly from the back of it. An agave needle. Distinctive not only for their poisonous properties, and for the tequila that came from the plant they protected, those needles were also sharp enough to puncture a throat. Or a boot heel.

There'd been a broken agave arm right by where the ranger had gone off the cliff the night before. The break hadn't been brand-new, clearly hadn't been a casualty of the ranger's death, but she'd sidestepped it to avoid being pricked by one of those needles...

Odin Rogers had been up on that mountain.

She couldn't prove it. Odin would say he'd stepped on the needle elsewhere. Agave plants could be from all over. She sure wouldn't be given a warrant to confiscate the boot based on a needle when she had no other proof that Odin Rogers was involved.

Her fellow officers might think, again, that she was too close to the case, was stretching reality to avenge her brother's death.

But she knew. Odin might not have killed her brother, but he was involved in whatever was going on up on that mountain. He was involved in having her brother killed.

For the moment, it was information she was going to keep to herself.

* * *

Rafe made it to his house and into the shower without anyone knowing he hadn't been home. And his privacy was one of the reasons he'd insisted on moving out of the mansion and into his own home. He'd never learned to be comfortable living with so many people coming and going and knowing who was coming and going.

In dark pants that had been hanging in his closetful of similar clothing—all bagged from the cleaners—a freshly laundered and pressed white shirt, and black-and-white tie, he arrived at Colton Oil fifteen minutes before the board meeting scheduled for ten that morning.

He'd hoped to have more to give the family regarding Payne's attempted murder. He also had a list of financials to go over with those of his siblings who were fellow board members and their ex-stepmother, Selina Barnes Colton, the firm's Vice President and Public Relations Director. Why Payne kept his ex-wife on the board, he had no idea, especially since Selina was a bit bitchy most of the time, but as with most things Payne Colton, it wasn't his job to question.

Still, he was dreading the meeting, when, generally, he got a bit of a kick out of them. Rafe, a foreman's son, sitting on the board of a billion-dollar company. Such an unlikely event. Just like him, the unlikely heir. He'd seen Payne's will. He wasn't set to inherit an amount equal to the rest of Payne's biological children, but he'd one day be a very rich man.

Richie Rich. Did whoever had thrown that brick in

Kerry's window that morning have something to do with shooting Payne?

The thought sickened him. As did the idea of having to sit through a Selina presentation that would be passing out edicts to them all regarding the presentation of Payne's shooting to whoever asked, in whatever manner she'd deemed best for the company. She was decent at her job. She just took far too much delight in ordering Payne's kids around.

He wasn't in the mood to take orders from anyone. Except Kerry Wilder.

All he really wanted to do was lie in the hammock he'd strung by the house, right in the place where he'd kissed Kerry the one and only time before last night, and relive the night he'd just spent in her bed. Going over and over every movement of her body, and his, every sensation. Cataloging them so he wouldn't ever lose one single second of those memories.

"Hey, Rafe." Marlowe, in all her petite, whitish-blond-haired beauty had arrived. The consummate professional. And one of his favorite siblings. He'd had a rough time the month before, when her life had been threatened. There'd been nothing he could do but watch out for her and trust that the guy would be caught. He'd always felt closer to Marlowe. As a kid, she'd been the one to seek his opinion at the dinner table. Offer him more potatoes. She'd not only supported him when he'd gone to Payne with his request to build his own place on RRR property, but she'd helped with some of the interior design choices, and getting things set up, too.

She'd visited his place the most over the years. He

couldn't be happier for her now that she was engaged to be married to a man she loved, and expecting her first child.

"Hey," he said, wanting to tell her that his entire world had changed. And at the same time not wanting anyone else to know.

She'd barely poured herself a cup of coffee before the others came in, each one bursting into the space with their own brand of arrival, and all with an eye to getting down to business.

It was Marlowe's first board meeting as CEO, but she handled the call to order as though she'd done it a million times before—nothing about her demeanor that morning would clue anyone in to the fact she was newly pregnant and newly engaged. She was all Colton.

The first order of business had been one they'd all been waiting for—a report from Colton Oil's IT specialist and department director, Daniel Okowski—about the mysterious email that had outed Ace to the board.

Rafe knew it wasn't going to be good when the man stood up and said, "I need to give you all a brief dark web rundown."

His fellow board members clearly shared his dread when they all looked at each other and then back at the tall, thin, black-spectacled man, who at thirty-eight was older than both Rafe and Marlowe.

"The dark web runs similar to the web with which you're all familiar, but using a specially encrypted software. One example is called Tor—which stands for The Onion Router—and is aptly named because what this software does is route everything that comes through it through different layers all over the world, making things virtually impossible to trace."

Rafe knew the news wasn't going to be good. Daniel went on to tell them that the email that had come into all of the board member's inboxes, telling them that Ace was not a biological Colton, had been sent through the dark web and had therefore been untraceable.

"Damn." He wasn't sure who, of the four seated board members, had whispered the word. Maybe Ainsley, second-oldest heir and Colton Oil's lead legal counsel. Could have been Marlowe or Selina, for all Rafe could tell. He just knew he seconded the sentiment.

And wished Ace was in the room. The man had his moments, but he was honest in his business dealings. And always knew how to keep things on an even keel. No matter what—at least in Rafe's opinion.

Based on Ace's outburst to his father after Payne had removed him from the board, Kerry and some of the others might not agree with his assessment.

"I move that this board track down the *real* Ace Colton." Selina didn't miss a beat.

Ainsley frowned, tapping a pen against the empty legal pad in front of her. Marlowe, after a brief, but clearly irritated, look at her ex-stepmother, looked to Rafe and Ainsley, "Do I have a second?"

They were two people short—Ace and Payne. Rafe felt the weight of their absence as he thought over Selina's declaration. Genevieve had Payne's proxy and they could get it if they needed it.

Looking for the real Colton heir opened a Pandora's

box that none of them, other than Selina, apparently, wanted unlocked. Not only was it disloyal to Ace, but according to Colton Oil bylaws, the CEO of the company had to be a biological heir. The real Ace could have legal grounds to come in and take over. Possibly try to change the company's direction. Take the money and run.

"I need a second for the motion before we can open the floor for discussion," Marlowe said.

"I second, but let the record show that it's only so that we can discuss," Ainsley said.

Fifteen minutes of Marlowe, Ainsley and Rafe trying to find a logical reason not to vote to hire someone to find the man who'd been switched as a baby with Ace, ended up with Marlowe calling for a vote and having it be unanimous. In favor of starting the search.

Ace was their brother. Their leader.

But someone else knew he wasn't a Colton. Someone knew more about them than they did. And it appeared that that someone had been willing to see Payne dead over the news.

They all knew Ace didn't shoot their father—even if they had no evidence.

And the fact that Payne was shot right on the heels of that email and the DNA test that had proven Ace not to be a biological Colton was too much of a coincidence for any of them to think that the two weren't related.

Since they couldn't find who sent the email, they were going to have to find who was behind the baby switching. Marlowe and Callum had already met with a hospital administrator, but the nursery and birth records from the day of the kidnapping had all been burned in the fire that broke out that long ago morning. So who knew that Ace wasn't the somewhat sickly child that Tessa Colton had given birth to that night in the wee hours before Christmas morning? And how did that information lead them to who wanted the Colton board to know that Ace wasn't really one of them?

Who wanted both Ace and Payne out of the way? And why?

Rafe had no answers.

But he fully believed they had to do whatever it took to find that person.

Just as he knew that he was going to give everything he had to helping Kerry find out who'd killed her brother.

After walking out on their love as he had, it was just something he had to do.

Chapter 9

After her meeting with Odin Rogers, Kerry spent some time digging into Marlowe Colton's life a bit more deeply, while she figured out her next move with Odin. Marlowe was known to be a workaholic. Was it possible she'd wanted to be CEO of Colton Oil so badly that she'd sent the email regarding Ace's parentage? But that didn't really make sense. If she'd known her brother wasn't a biological Colton, she could simply have told her father discreetly and asked for a DNA test. Or given him what proof she had.

So she hadn't known about Ace, but when they'd found out, she'd assumed she'd be named CEO. Perhaps she had been pissed that Payne had temporarily appointed himself to take Ace's place before naming her to the position. So she'd shot her father?

But she had an alibi—her brand-new fiancé, Bowie Robertson. They'd been at his place. Making love, in case anyone wanted to run forensics. Or so she'd been told. She didn't figure she'd get a warrant for those bodily fluids. Or get any proof even if she did, considering the time that had passed.

Nothing in any of the records she could search showed Marlowe to be anything but what she appeared, and from what Kerry had witnessed the night she'd barged into their family grieving session to bring in Ace for questioning, Marlowe had been hit hard by the shooting. Nothing, past or present, showed someone who'd resort to violence. She'd never even had a speeding ticket.

So she was on the bottom of the suspect list. Still there, but at the tail end.

Kerry's list of leads was dismal. There were some forensics that she was still waiting on. She'd received a report on the bullet that had hit Payne. It was a common bullet from a common gun that was sold regularly—meaning any of a thousand people could have purchased it legally just in their part of the state and just in the past year.

And her shooter could have come by it illegally. She spent time looking at reports of guns stolen, cross-referenced them to anyone who seemed to have any link with the Coltons but so far had come up empty. And she looked for recent sales of ammunition, came up with several just in their area south of Tucson, but, again, nothing hit with any cross-reference searches.

Still, she'd spend the hours it took to follow up on all of the names, just in case.

And she kept thinking about Odin Rogers. Had to know what the man was up to. He sure as hell wouldn't just be sitting around watching TV all day or spending his days investing money. Who did he see? Where did he hang out? What was he up to, right then, while she sat at her desk at the police station, looking for one particular gun in a sea of thousands?

There'd been known associates over the years, but Odin didn't seem to keep many people around long. The MVPD had talked to many of them, had been able to arrest a few on small charges, but nothing that led them anywhere.

So she thought about what she did know. From her wall. From Tyler. Thinking about the mountain.

What she didn't do was allow herself to drift off to thoughts of Rafe. Or the night she'd spent with him. That little treasure was hers to cherish. But only when she was alone. And off work.

For the moment, she was able to push it away every time it zoomed forward, which was way too often. Somewhat because her body was feeling the aftermath of so much lovemaking. It had been a while for her. Physical moment brought instant reminder.

As soon as Dane, who was officially looking into the ranger's death, had left for the day, Kerry did, too. In her own Jeep, and without telling anyone what she was doing, she headed back toward Rogers's neighborhood. Just to see.

If she knew where he went, who he saw, she'd be better able to find a clue that would piece everything together. Something that officially linked Tyler and Rogers. Or Rogers and the ranger, at least.

She didn't even make it to his place. Half a mile away, she saw his truck pull around a corner and head away from town. She wouldn't be able to follow him if he continued on, not directly. On a road where there was nothing to look at except for whatever vehicles might be in front of or behind you, he'd be sure to see her. But she could stick with him just long enough to see if he was headed toward the mountain. And then call Dane.

She almost missed Rogers's turn off the main drive out of town, just a few blocks before leaving the town behind. Taking one street sooner, she made a quick second turn and ended up facing the road he was on just after he drove past her intersection. Good. He wouldn't have seen her.

She let another car pass, and then pulled out behind it, keeping her distance, hoping the old gray truck stayed on the road as far as Odin did, giving her some cover. She could see Odin's truck through the windshield of the truck between them, but didn't figure he'd be able to make her out. He'd know her vehicle—not from their visit that morning, but from the mountain the night before.

Unless he'd hired someone to watch the mountain, and the ranger. Which actually made more sense. He'd have henchmen. She was pretty sure she could name one or two of them, not that she'd been able to get enough intel to be sure. It wasn't like she was officially investigating or had any right to go questioning people about the man.

No, she was on the Colton case.

The ranger's death was Dane's.

When Odin turned again, she felt that tiny thrill of

excitement that came when she was close to getting somewhere on a case. He'd turned right instead of left this time. Not going in a circle.

Could be he'd spotted her, was giving her the runaround, but she didn't think so. He wasn't varying his speed.

And the man was probably just cocky enough to figure he could get away with anything he chose to do so wouldn't bother with worrying about surveillance.

He'd been smart enough to get away with a life of slimeball crime for years, she reminded herself. Her mistake would be to underestimate him.

As she approached the road where Odin had turned off—a gravelly lane that led through a run-down neighborhood filled with old cars, broken gates on scarred stucco walls, homes in disrepair and yards with no landscaping—she drove slowly past so she could get a look at what he was doing. He'd slowed outside a house and she made a quick U-turn, pulling off to the shoulder, just before the intersection. She could see Odin and not be seen.

A minute or so later a beat-up black sedan with a dented front bumper and cardboard where the front passenger window should have been pulled out of a drive farther down the road and approached Rogers, slowing as the car came up alongside. She couldn't tell what the vehicle's occupants were doing, but the two vehicles sat there, side by side, for a good minute before the sedan started forward again, and Odin, turning in a driveway, followed behind it.

Kerry turned quickly, making it to the next block before either of them made it to the end of their street, and was turned around and ready to pull out behind them as they left. Tapping her steering wheel as she waited impatiently for another vehicle to drive up behind them so she could turn out, she almost lost them, but caught up before they reached Mustang Boulevard. Odin turned back toward town, but the car he'd met— obviously with a particular mission, since he was now headed back the way he'd come—headed out of town.

Straight toward the mountain.

She had a choice to make. Call Dane, hoping that her fellow detective would see merit in Odin's meeting and head out to actually find the car she had her eye on, or make certain that she found out what was going on by following the guy herself. No brainer there.

But remembering the night before, the ranger's death, the attempt on her life, the warning she'd received that morning, she knew she couldn't head up the mountain without someone knowing where she was. If she called the station, she'd be told to stand down. The case wasn't hers. And she'd already been targeted.

And that was the only reason she texted Rafe. He was the only other person who knew what was going on. And she trusted him not to get in the way of her need to bring Tyler's killer to justice.

After that, she was all business, staying far enough behind the old car that she almost lost it a couple of times. Going slow to ensure that other cars pulled in between them on the long open road. And when they reached the mountain road, she pulled off anytime she thought she'd be visible, waiting at turns, taking it slowly. So much so that she almost missed that the car had stopped, pulling off into some brush on a flat piece of land that butted up to the cliff.

Kerry continued on up the mountain until she could turn around, and then as quickly as she could, retraced the route, passing the parked car and heading down just until she found a place where she could somewhat hide the Jeep. Getting out she hiked the quarter mile back to where she'd seen the car. And then, picking each step carefully, tried to catch sight of the guy, to figure out where he'd gone, without alerting him that she was there. At least she didn't have to worry about rattlesnakes. It would be another three months before they'd be out sunning themselves again.

The phone in the holster attached to her hip vibrated. Once. Text message, not a call. Could be from anyone at the station. One of the friends she and Lizzie hung out with at the bar in town on occasion. Or Rafe.

Any or all of them would have to wait. Still, it was… nice…to feel the presence of someone she knew as she ventured off into a potentially dangerous unknown.

It didn't take her long to find the guy. Probably because he didn't know he was being followed and, unlike her, he wasn't choosing his steps carefully. Dressed all in black, with dark hair and a beard, he was plodding in black work boots up what she could see now was a trail carved around the side of the mountain, leading gradually up to…something.

A cave? The place where Rogers stashed his guns and drugs? Or both?

Heart pounding, she held back a second, focused on the sounds he was making, keeping herself close enough to hear him without being seen. Stopping when she came to flat pieces of land with cliff overhang above her, little hiding places that allowed her to let him get far enough ahead of her that he wouldn't discover that she was behind him.

Adrenaline poured through her. Two years of yearning, of studying, investigating, knowing, and she was finally starting to get some answers. If it hadn't been for the ranger's rudeness the night before, and then the attempt made to run her off the road, alerting her to the fact that she wasn't wanted up on the mountain, she'd never have known that she was onto something.

The chief always said that everyone made mistakes and sometimes cracking a case meant waiting for the perp to make his.

Standing at a jutted-out piece of the face of the mountain, half hiding behind it, Kerry listened. She couldn't hear the thug—or a perfectly nice guy who just happened to know Odin Rogers and hang out at the site of a murder from the night before—and couldn't move until sound alerted her to his whereabouts. He could, at any time, head back down the mountain and if he did, she had to make damned sure he didn't find her.

Looking around for an alcove big enough for her to fit in, she noticed a pile of tumbleweeds off to her left. They generally blew and conglomerated in places where they got stuck—an inlay? Looking around the craggy mountainside, to see if she could make out any indication that anyone was coming back down, she turned, thinking she'd hide for a minute or two, just in case, maybe check her phone to see if she had service...

Before she could move, blinding pain struck the back of her skull.

* * *

Rafe had had no problem finding Kerry's car. From there he had no idea where to go, but figured up was more likely than down so he headed up the road, keeping to the mountain side, looking for any sign of underbrush that had been broken down recently, stepped on. Listening for any sign of human habitation.

Was he too late?

No way was he going to be too late.

As soon as he'd gotten her text he'd headed out of the office, and into a clothing store half a block away. Bought the first pair of jeans and tennis shoes he could find in his size, and wore them out of the store, carrying his pants and dress shoes with him.

He thought he heard a rock drop. Stopped. Listened, and then saw an old, beat-up black car pulled off into an alcove on the side of the mountain. Instinct told him Kerry would have seen it, too, and he headed in that direction. It didn't take him long to find the trail that led up the back of the mountain.

Could just be a hiker out there. It wasn't uncommon, especially with January being the beginning of hiking season, but something was telling him that Kerry needed him.

Or maybe he just needed her to need him.

Wanted her to need him.

He'd gone a quarter of a mile up the trail when he heard a sound that gave him a sickening feeling. Maybe a startled yelp. *Human*, he thought. But a large thump, too. Like something had been dropped, as opposed to sliding rubble.

Visions of the brick thrown through Kerry's front

window that morning had him racing toward the sound. Whoever was out there would hear him, but he figured that couldn't be bad at the moment. Not if the distraction saved Kerry's life.

Could be she'd just slipped.

Might not have been her he heard at all. His feet raced forward anyway, sliding on the mountainside as he veered off the uneven path, taking shortcuts wherever he found them.

He saw her a couple of minutes later, lying in an unmoving lump on the ground—several yards below him. He'd gone too far.

Movement off to his left alerted him he wasn't alone just as a hunk of black came sailing toward him.

"What did you do to her?" he yelled as he caught the flying weight and threw it down to the ground. Thank God for the karate lessons he'd taken to spite Payne during college. The man, all in black, was easily fifty pounds heavier than Rafe, but the anger fueled energy flowing through him, and the heavy landing with the man's own weight working against him, gave Rafe the upper hand. If this man had killed Kerry, he wasn't getting off the mountain alive.

He punched. And punched again. With every bit of force in him, he kept attacking until he realized that the other man wasn't fighting back. He didn't know if he'd killed his opponent, or just knocked him out, but left him on the ground there as he raced toward the body lying so still down below.

God, let her still be breathing. She had to still be breathing.

If she wasn't …

She *was* breathing. He could discern the small up-and-down movement of her chest while he was still several feet away.

"Kerry," he called, aware that the guy up above them could regain consciousness at any moment.

She moaned. Blinked. Then lay still again.

"It's okay, Ker," he said softly, not sure if he was crying or not. Hoped not. Suddenly, he was thirteen again, being forced to stay in his room and watch the person he loved most in the world heading out to their hill all alone.

Crying as he knew he'd lost her.

They were the last years he could remember shedding tears…

He felt for her pulse as soon as he reached her. Let out a breath as he felt the strong beat.

"Okay, I'm going to lift you, sweetie. I hope it doesn't hurt, but I have to get you off this mountain."

Her lashes fluttered once more, but she didn't open her eyes again.

Rafe wasn't going to worry about that yet. He'd seen a small stain of blood on the ground as he lifted Kerry's head. There was a gash on the back of her skull. With all her hair, he couldn't tell how bad it was, but figured that the man up above had dropped something down on her. Probably a rock. He didn't take the time to find out which one of the many ones around them could have been the one. Taking off his belt to tie her to him, he wrapped one arm around her and used the other to balance them both as he half climbed, half slid down the mountain.

Chapter 10

Her head hurt. Kerry turned, easing the pain, and opened her eyes to see Rafe sitting in a chair, leaning in close, watching her.

She'd been in the emergency room for hours, having to wait until the tests came back that would tell them that, other than the surface pain which was completely manageable, she was as fine as she'd said she was. She wasn't feeling drunk. Her thinking was clear and quick. She was bristling at the inactivity while Odin Rogers's thug had a chance to get away.

And was pretending to doze, too, so that she didn't have to converse with the man who'd just risked his own life to save hers. Didn't trust herself to speak to him while the intense emotions his actions had raised in her were still so raw. Didn't want him to see how much he meant to her. Not when she didn't trust him to always be there for her. Not when his being there for her that day made those times when he wasn't hurt so much more. He had a scrape on the side of his chin. And some blistered knuckles, too, she'd noticed when he'd thought she was resting and had been talking to one of the technicians who'd come into their little white-curtained cubicle.

She'd heard Rafe's voice, and then the scuffle above her on the mountain, had just wanted to be able to sleep for a few minutes, until her head stopped hurting, but had known, too, that she had to fight to stay conscious. So she'd lain completely still, praying the pain would subside so she could be sure she wouldn't pass out if she stood up.

And then Rafe had been there and she'd focused on the soft tones of his voice, rested against him as he'd carried her off the mountain. She'd looked at him and smiled a thank-you when he strapped her into the front seat of his truck and then kept her eyes closed the rest of the way to the hospital.

"If he'd been just an inch over, he'd have caught you on the back of the skull and could have killed you." His voice in that small cubicle was low, but didn't hide the intensity behind the words as he noticed her watching him.

She gave a very small nod. "The guy who did the CT scan said that the full weight of the boulder just skimmed the back point of my skull." It had been enough to stun her, knock her over. They weren't sure if it was the fall or the rock that knocked her out.

She hadn't even needed stitches. Or to have her hair shaved, thank goodness.

She'd only lost consciousness for a few seconds, a minute at most, they figured, based on how soon Rafe came upon the guy and her ability to hear him up there beating the guy to a pulp.

"I'm just pissed he got away," she said. The chief had been in to see her. And to tell her that by the time Dane got to the mountain, the black car was gone and there was no sign of any man, dead or alive, up above the car. He'd collected the rock that was used to hit her. It was close to where the small pool of her blood had been and had a tiny bit of blood on it. Probably hers. If they were lucky, they'd get prints from it.

They'd brought her Jeep back to the station and put out a notice on the black car, which had so far netted nothing. Kerry had written down the license and they'd done a search to find the car was reported totaled two years before and sent to a scrap yard.

Rafe hadn't gotten a good look at the man's face and neither had Kerry. But she remembered he was big. Had a beard, which he could easily shave, and dark hair. Chief Barco had asked, and no one matching that description had come into the hospital, or any of the clinics in town, seeking medical attention for a pummeling, but anyone could have taken him into Tucson. Or even up to Phoenix.

And Dane had gone to the house where she'd seen the car pull out of the driveway, but the woman who answered the door said she didn't know anyone by the man's description, that she'd been at the house alone with her elderly mother all day and that she didn't recognize the car. She suggested it could have been turning around in her driveway. She showed the detective the green hatchback she had parked in her garage and the plates came back registered to her.

Whether she was covering for the thug, or had been telling the truth, they were no closer to finding out who the man was, why he'd met with Odin, and what he was doing up on that mountain.

"I'm going back up there," she told Rafe.

"I know." He looked so serious, sitting there in his stained shirt, with his tie still knotted at his throat, and jeans and tennis shoes.

He looked approachable. More like a guy who'd hang out in the same general world she inhabited, rather than a member of the privileged wealthy.

Leaning forward again, his elbows on his knees and his bruised hands clasped, he glanced at her. "I need you to promise me that you won't go back up there alone," he said, frowning as though preparing for an argument.

Leading her to want to say, "Make me," like the kid she'd once been would have said to the kid he'd once been when a dare had been issued.

But the truth was, he probably *could* make her. He could hire someone to watch her, to follow her. Hell, he could probably have her boss put her on permanent leave, forcing her to move out of Mustang Valley if she wanted to work.

Recognizing the ridiculousness of the thought, Kerry also knew there was truth in it. The Coltons really were that powerful in Mustang Valley.

Still…

"I have to, Rafe," she told him. Because she couldn't afford to hire her own goon. "If the chief knows I'm going, he'll order me not to do so."

"I know."

He probably knew that the chief figured she'd be back up on that mountain, too. He didn't try to stop her from doing what she had to do. Unless she made an official request that would force him to do so.

So, the promise request? That had just been for show?

"That's why I'm going with you," he told her. "I'm already in as far as anyone could get, I've not only been seen, but I've now beat someone unconscious. And I'm going to see this through, Kerry."

He wasn't going to let this go. Or leave her alone, either, until Tyler's murder was solved. And truth was, she had a better chance at success with his help. As proven by his actions that afternoon. If he hadn't come running as soon as he'd gotten her text...

She'd have lain there until the thug was gone and then gotten herself off the mountain. Or pretended to be dead until he got close enough for her to shoot him.

But it could have gone badly, too. She could have been dizzy. Missed her shot. And ended up in a gully just like her brother and the ranger.

"Okay," she said softly.

"Okay? You're not just saying that because you think it will get me off your back on this, are you?"

"No." She looked him right in the eye. "I'm saying it because I want to find out who killed my brother. I can't tell the chief what I'm doing and get official help, and I can't afford to hire anyone to help."

He nodded. Sat back. Gave her the first smile she'd seen on his grim face since he'd made love to her the night before.

And then, bringing his chair closer, he took her hand, his expression serious again. "I won't let you down again, Kerry. I'll always be here for you."

Her heart slammed shut. "No, you won't be," she said, just as softly. "Please, Rafe, please don't make promises you can't keep."

"I…"

She shook her head twice, back and forth, in spite of the pain. "I mean it, Rafe. I need you to agree that there will be no promises between us. Because we both know that as soon as Payne gains consciousness, as soon as your life gets back to normal, our paths won't be crossing again."

She wanted him to deny her declaration. To give her some hope that there could be a possibility of a miracle in their future. Someday. That he'd leave his family and their wealth and come into town to live with her.

Because they both knew Payne would never accept her at the family dinner table at the RRR. Or in Rafe's house, either.

When he said nothing, she had her answer.

Rafe went upstairs to see Payne while Kerry's physician was in with her. He was her ride home; he knew she wouldn't leave without him, but still, he was on edge leaving her.

Not good. Or healthy. And one of the reasons he left her. That, and because of his late shower followed by the board meeting and his need to get some other time sensitive things done in the office, he'd missed his morning visit with the older man.

Genevieve was sitting alone in the room and smiled when Rafe came in, accepting his invitation to be with Payne while she went to the cafeteria for a snack.

"How you doing?" he asked the elder Colton as he took a seat close to the bed. The doctor had told them there was every chance the comatose Payne could hear them talk, encouraging them to do so, and Rafe took the opportunity to tell his adoptive father how much it hurt him to lose his oldest friend in the world. He talked about what Kerry had meant to him as a five-year-old, and as a thirteen-year-old, too. He told Payne that he didn't think it was any mistake that she'd been assigned to his case. He didn't vent. Didn't place blame. He just talked, stopping short of admitting to any current relationship with his ex-friend. He wasn't ready to go there.

To put limits on it.

Or add a definition to it.

The talk wasn't all that long; Genevieve returned quickly and Rafe had to get back downstairs to Kerry, not that he told his stepmother that he had any other purpose at the hospital. If she noticed the scrape on the side of his jaw, she didn't mention it.

Nor did she ask why he was in jeans.

Because she didn't notice enough about him to know the dress was unusual? Didn't care? Or was just too upset about Payne to bother with anything else? He didn't know.

She didn't ask about the morning's board meeting. Chances were Marlowe, who was her daughter, had already been to the hospital and filled her in.

Nothing had changed as he rode the elevator back down, but he felt better, nonetheless. Didn't matter whether Payne heard the words or not; he'd needed to tell his father how he felt.

Kerry was fully dressed, disconnected from all hospital monitors and sitting in the chair he'd vacated, when he returned to her cubicle.

"No internal bleeding, not even any brain swelling," she said as soon as he pushed through the curtain. She stood, reaching for the gun that the chief had taken from her holster when he'd visited her earlier, and then, not finding it, frowned. "Can you just drop me at the station?" she asked. "I need to get my Jeep and my gun."

He planned to follow her home, too. To make sure she didn't have any problems driving, not that he told her so.

"I was thinking, maybe since we're here, we could ask around for some long-term employees, see if anyone remembers the fire from forty years ago, or knows who was working in maternity back then. Or knows someone who would know. If we can't find Payne's shooter in one way, we'll go about it another."

He stopped at the end of the bed. "You know that the email couldn't be traced?"

"Ainsley left a message late this morning," she said. As Colton Oil's attorney, Ainsley's choice made sense. Rafe just didn't like not being the one who gave Kerry Colton news.

He'd been sitting at that table. Had voted on the motion.

"I actually would like to question employees," he said, "but I think we should wait until tomorrow." When she looked ready to argue he glanced at her clothes. Her hair. And down at himself. "I think we'd get a better response after a shower and some rest."

For once, she didn't argue with him.

Or have a better idea.

"Detective! Detective Wilder!"

Kerry was just getting into her car at the station after a brief talk with the chief and Dane—assuring them both she was fine and would be at her desk in the morning, and retrieving the gun and cell phone the chief had taken into safe custody when he'd seen her at the hospital—when someone called her name from behind. Called it loudly. Demandingly.

Turning she noticed three things at once. Rafe's truck was still where he'd parked it when he dropped her off. He was getting out of it and approaching her. And from a slightly different direction, so was Ace Colton.

"Mr. Colton," she addressed Ace, ignoring Rafe's presence for the moment, not sure whose side he was on for this conversation. Thinking he might have told Ace where to find her. "What can I do for you?"

"What can you do for me?" The forty-year-old intimidating man asked. Tall and leanly muscled, Ace had a reputation for being somewhat ruthless. Kerry wasn't the least bit intimidated. Even after the day she'd had.

"That's what I asked," she said. "Did you need something?"

"Yeah, I need something." The man, in a suit coat and tie, glanced at Rafe, almost as though just noticing he was there, and then back at Kerry. "You can tell me what's going on with my father's case. Three nights ago you haul me away from my family, while we're all still in shock, you make me call my lawyer away from his family, ask me a bunch of questions, tell me not to leave town, and then…nothing."

"When I have something to tell you, or need anything from you, I'll let you know," she said. "The investigation is ongoing."

Still not allowing herself to look at Rafe, she faced the ousted CEO with complete calm. Ace Colton had never been a threat to her. Only his father had been. Or rather, his supposed father. Truth be known, she kind of felt for the guy. Thinking he was one thing all his life, an elevated, important and very rich something, only to find that he might be as low as Kerry— the hired help.

She felt the sting of that distinction very clearly.

Could definitely relate.

"Can you at least tell me if I'm a suspect?" he asked. "I'd like to be free to head to Tucson if I choose to do so."

While Ace had been removed from the Colton board, she assumed he was still working at the company. It wasn't like all he did all day was sign CEO papers. But she could be wrong about that.

"At this time I can tell you that the investigation is ongoing and you've been advised not to leave town."

"You're wasting Mustang Valley Police Department time. You realize that, I hope."

She wasn't going to let him see that his insulting tone, more than his words, stung. Especially with Rafe standing right there, in between them, but closer to Ace than to her.

"You have no idea how I'm spending my time," she

blurted, and then hated that she'd done so. That she'd let him get to her. And wouldn't the high-and-mighty Ace Colton like to know just what she'd been doing with her time the night before. All night long.

Of course, he might already know. News tended to travel fast in Mustang Valley. But from what she'd understood, news of the townspeople didn't often reach the elegant offices of Colton Oil. Their interests were outside Mustang Valley.

But even if the Coltons had heard that Rafe spent the night at her house, she had said that he'd slept on the couch. She was pretty sure even the chief believed that one.

Who, knowing Kerry, wouldn't? She wasn't the type to do something stupid like fall for someone so far out of her league.

And she lived and breathed police work.

She was married to her job.

"Are you listening to me?" Ace's words stopped her racing thoughts. "I did not shoot my father. I don't even own a gun."

True about the gun. But the crime files were filled with murderers who didn't own guns. At least not legally.

"He didn't do it, Kerry." Rafe chose one hell of a time to speak up. On Ace's side, of course. "I *know* him. He can be a bit of an ass, but he's not a killer. None of us are."

The defense made her mad. Or hurt. She wasn't sure which. She just knew that her response was reactionary even before it was out of her mouth.

"Yes, Ace, you are a suspect," she said. Taking what power she could from both of them. "You were heard to say, and admitted in front of counsel and on tape, that you threatened Payne Colton shortly before he was shot, which is motive, and you have no alibi. I don't have any hard evidence that will prove you did this—yet. I'm still waiting for some reports to come back. I've got other things I'm checking—tapes I'm looking at, people I'm talking to—and if Payne regains consciousness, he might remember something, too."

"Let me tell you this," Rafe said. "If Ace was supposedly in town and at the office, rather than at the ranch, someone would have seen it. Or it would have been on a surveillance camera."

That was one of the things she was still checking. "Not necessarily," she said. "He could have caught a ride into town in any number of ways, if he'd wanted to do so unseen. And most everybody in town knows where security cameras are positioned. He could have made sure he avoided them."

It was one of the problems of small towns—people knowing who had security and who didn't.

"But there was nothing on Colton Oil security footage showing him either entering or leaving the building."

"It didn't show anyone else entering the building, either," she quickly pointed out.

"Give it up, Rafe," Ace said with one last half sneer at her, and then turned to the man Kerry had just slept with. "But thanks for the vote of confidence. It means a lot."

She had to stand there and watch as the older man gripped the back of Rafe's shoulder and the two men clasped arms and embraced.

A brother thing.

Chapter 11

Rafe followed Kerry home and then, without even getting out of his truck, waved goodbye to her as she pulled into her garage.

Ace's visit had upset her. He got that. Understood why. Empathized. And couldn't change it.

The visit didn't change his plan for the evening, nor the fact that he was going to do his best to make it hard for her to argue with him. Outside of Colton Oil business, he didn't use his family's weight to get what he wanted, but he was going to make an exception that night.

He was in and out of his house at the ranch in five minutes, getting together an overnight bag and clothes for work the next day, and was already headed back into town when he made his first phone call.

He'd used Jason Wendt as a PI once before, when

Payne had first appointed Selina to the board. The others might have done their own checking into their father's affairs, but Rafe had needed to make certain, from a purely Colton Oil financial security aspect, that the woman wasn't bribing Payne.

Nothing else had ever made sense. The woman could barely tolerate any of Payne's offspring, him included. She was rude and generally unpleasant to be around. And Payne let her live in a house on the property. Jason had found a few interesting skeletons in Selina's closet, but nothing to do with Payne. Nothing to even hint at anything she might have over him.

He'd cringed a time or two, reading the details on Selina's life—but he had been immensely impressed with Jason's thoroughness.

"Rafe, good to hear from you." The man picked up on the second ring.

He didn't waste time with pleasantries. He needed the man on Odin Rogers, starting immediately, no cost spared. He wanted Jason to look as deep as one could look, go wherever he had to go, if necessary, hire whoever he needed to hire, and keep him posted with every update, or every twelve hours if there was nothing new.

He wasn't even halfway into town when that call disconnected. And then he called Shelly Marston, the government attorney he'd once slept with after closing a drilling deal, only to find out later that she was married, to see if his call to her that morning had vetted anything on Grant Alvin.

She had nothing of use to give him and he hung up.

He chafed the rest of the way back to Kerry's neighborhood, just needing to be there. To know that she was safe. She'd rejected her chief's offer of another night of squad car protection outside her home. Whoever was out there wasn't committing crimes in town. As long as she stayed home, she'd be okay.

What that told Rafe was that she didn't yet know what they didn't want her to know. And that whatever it was, was up on that mountain. She'd been warned, severely, twice now, to stay off that mountain.

And she wasn't going to do so.

The thought made him shaky.

One street over from her house he made his third call. She picked up on the first ring. A good sign.

"Do you ever park your Jeep in your driveway overnight?"

"I have before," she said. "Why?"

"Because I think you should again tonight."

"Okay, why?"

"Because it would be best to park my truck in the garage so tongues don't start to wag."

"What? You are not spending the night here again, Rafe. Last night…it was a one-shot deal. We both agreed."

"Don't get your panties in a wad…" He stopped. Couldn't believe he'd said anything so crass. Especially to her.

She brought out the little boy in him. The one who'd lived before Payne Colton got a hold of him.

"I apologize… I am not assuming that I have a place in your bed, nor am I asking for one," he told her. "The couch will be fine. You have a concussion, and yes the doctor released you, but I would rather you not be alone. I'd set your alarm for every two hours, just to make sure there are no adverse reactions to the concussion. I know the doctor only suggested it as a precaution, and only because you asked, but, seriously, who would know if you don't wake up?"

"My friend Lizzie. She insisted on staying, but gave in when I told her I'd text her if I needed her."

Rafe knew he should have perhaps considered that she had a support system. A tribe that didn't include him.

"I thought maybe we could go over aerial maps of the mountain, homing in on the area where we know the guy was headed today, and see what we can find. I'd like to have a solid plan before we head up and I suspect we're heading up tomorrow, as soon as you're off work."

She'd given her word she'd take him with her. But he knew her well enough to know that if he wasn't available when she was ready to go, she'd take that to mean he was letting her out of the deal.

"I don't think…"

"I'm not leaving you alone tonight," he said. "If you won't take me, I've got a guy on hold to at least watch your house."

He'd mentioned to Jason that he might need a second guy. Just for the night.

"Fine. I'll move the Jeep. How long until you get here?"

"Sixty seconds." He pulled around the corner onto her street.

And wiped the grin off his face.

She didn't want Rafe in her space. At the moment, Kerry just wanted to be alone. It was the only way she knew how to deal with pain. Grief. Fear. Confusion.

From the time she was thirteen she'd done it all

alone. Her dad hadn't been well enough to be a support to her. And Tyler, she'd always put on a brave face for him. Looking out for him, not vice versa.

Having Rafe just suddenly show up—and strong-arm her into letting him in by threatening to do something he knew she'd hate, and something he knew she knew he'd do—should have made her royally pissed.

Instead, she was kind of amused by his transparent tactics. And a bit moved by his motive. He was really worried about her.

It didn't mean anything life changing. But still, it was nice.

Which was the only reason she had a smile on her face when she opened her door to him. Still in the jeans and tennis shoes he'd had on earlier, he came in carrying an overnight duffel on a strap over his shoulder.

And a hanger filled with dress shirt, pants and a tie.

It wasn't that she was thinking his visit meant anything permanent, or signified any change between them. It just felt good to know that he was worried about her.

"Wow, they did a good job," he said, nodding toward the front room. "You can't even tell it's a new window."

She could. The old one had had a moisture cloud between the panes on the left-middle side.

"You can hang those in the closet in the spare room," she said. "There's no bed in there, just my desk, but there's an inflatable mattress if you'd rather use that instead of the couch."

Because his being there was not for them to sleep together again. He'd said it. And she needed that fact clearly established from the beginning.

No way was she going to spend the evening wondering. Wanting. Talking herself into one more night of pretending heaven on earth was real.

"I've called up aerial maps," she said as soon as Rafe came walking back down the hall minus his bag. In the jeans and T-shirt she'd changed into after her shower, she was leaning over her personal tablet and her department-issued laptop placed side by side on the dining room table.

"I was hoping I could take a shower first?" he said. She looked up to see flannel pants and a T-shirt in his hands. "I didn't want to take the time to shower at home…"

Because he was worried about her and eager to get back.

"Fine," she said. "You can use the spare bathroom in the hall. There's a set of towels under the sink." And in the meantime she was going to brew herself some peppermint tea, and on her way to do that, she went down the hall, past the spare bath where she could hear the shower start, and in to get her lavender oil. Both were good for headaches. And lavender was calming, too.

The shower was still running on her way back to the kitchen. No big deal. She'd had guests before. Had them shower in her bathroom. She just hadn't ever pictured them actually in the act, completely naked, with soap suds on their…

No. She had to stop.

The image of Rafe's penis was just fresh in her mind. Because of the night before. That was all. She wasn't losing it.

Or, if she was, it was just the crack on the head. She'd be over it in the morning.

Or sooner. Did peppermint and lavender take care of unwanted sensual thoughts, too?

Her tea was not only brewed, but half-gone by the time Rafe was back in the dining room. She'd been studying the aerial photos—satellite images that were readily available on the internet these days.

She could get Odin Rogers without Rafe's help, but she had a better chance of doing it and staying alive if she had backup. The afternoon's events had shown her that much. If she hadn't texted Rafe, she could have died out on that mountain. And it was clear to her that Dane was going to focus on solving the ranger's death, not on catching Odin Rogers. She knew his investigation was going to lead him there eventually, unless they wrote this one off as an accident, too, but she wasn't going to sit around and wait.

Something was going on; the perpetrators were nervous about her sniffing around, which meant now was the time to sniff harder.

She was smart to let Rafe help her do that.

Besides, he kind of owed it to Tyler. And to her.

One glance at those dark plaid flannel pants, and the T-shirt stretched over the expanse of flesh, and she was reaching for the tea again. She told herself he most definitely had underwear on beneath the pants.

And if he didn't, she'd never know about it.

But Rafe would make certain that he had something to hold on to his hard-on. If he got one.

Would he get one?

Being alone in her home with her all night?

Did she have at least that little bit of an effect on him?

"So...here are the aerial maps," she said, tapping

on her laptop to wake it up. And then repeating the process with her tablet. "I'm thinking we were right about here…" Using the mouse, she moved the pointer, stepping over a few inches as Rafe came closer, leaned down, to study the screen.

His hair was still wet. She'd seen it that way as kids, when they'd play in the landscape sprinklers when one sprung a leak, or turn the hose on each other. As an adult—all that blond thickness…

She stepped back. A good two feet. "Can I get you something to drink?" she asked. "I've got tea, or we can brew some coffee." She had wine, too, but she wasn't offering any.

"Coffee would be great. If you'd like we can order some dinner from Lucia's or Mustang Valley Steak and Seafood…they'll both deliver…"

She'd planned to have salad for dinner. Just wasn't that hungry. But if they ordered in, eating and cleaning up would give them something to do besides his standing there trying to work while she panted after him.

She was supposed to be sniffing, not panting. Around Odin Rogers, not Rafe Colton. And what was with the dog metaphors? She needed to get a serious grip.

"Lucia's sounds good," she said. Pasta would sit easier than a rich, heavy dinner.

Of course he had the restaurant on speed dial, but…

"Wait," she said. "Let me call. The family dinner is a good deal and I've ordered it before and take the rest to work for lunches. We don't want anyone knowing you're here," she reminded him. She didn't, at least. Probably wouldn't hurt Rafe Colton's reputation to go slumming with the detective investigating his father's attempted murder, but she didn't want townspeople to think she was the type of woman who got her head turned by a heavy wallet. Or to have them feeling sorry for her for being stupid enough to think that a Colton would give her more than a passing moment.

By the time she'd ordered dinner she had herself back under control. Maybe the peppermint and lavender had kicked in. Maybe she just came to her senses.

Either way, there was going to be no sex in her house that night.

Rafe was thoroughly enjoying himself. Dressed like he dressed on Saturday or Sunday mornings when he knew he was going to be home alone, he felt at home. Relaxed.

He'd told her he'd sleep on the couch. He didn't expect her to really make him do so. Though, if she really wanted him to, he would. Without question.

As they sat there eating dinner, discussing Odin Rogers and different theories about the day's activities, he didn't even care if they made love that night or not. He was just glad to be the one who was watching out for her. To be with her at all.

To see her smile.

And watch her eat.

"Sorry about Ace today," he said. He'd been waiting for a good moment to bring it up. Figured there wasn't one. But she hadn't looked him in the eye, really looked, since they'd left the hospital. And the only thing that he could think of that had happened in between then and now, as far as they were concerned, was when Ace confronted her.

She shrugged, twirled some spaghetti around her fork. "No need to apologize," she said, taking the bite. Finishing it. "Dealing with suspects is all in a day's work."

It had been more than that. He'd caught a glimpse of her face over Ace's shoulder when his brother had hugged him. Funny how, now that Ace wasn't a biological Colton either, he suddenly felt closer to the guy.

Another outsider on the inside.

Kerry wasn't on the inside. Never would be. And that hug had shown her how opposite their worlds really were. Their circumstances hadn't changed any from that moment, at the hospital, or the night before, or twenty-three years ago.

They were who they were.

"I've noticed, you don't always call Payne 'Dad.' Or mention him as 'my father.' Why is that?"

She glanced over at him, and then went back to eating.

He'd never really felt like a true Colton. Not completely. And Payne had acted more like a guardian than a father to him.

"I had a father," he said. "I have great memories of him. I still miss him. Payne never tried to take his place." And that was all he was going to say about that.

Chapter 12

"I looked my mother up." Kerry didn't think it was a good idea to say the words. She just wanted to. She'd asked about Payne because she was being kind of mean. Trying to point out that Rafe had chosen to stay with a family that wasn't really family to him all those years ago.

But the hug she'd witnessed between him and Ace had shown her that they *were* family.

She wasn't proud of herself.

Or happy about the fact that she'd deliberately tried to hurt him. That wasn't her way, never had been, and it wasn't going to start now.

Rafe had swallowed his bite of lasagna and was looking at her.

"Your mother? You found her? When?"

His eyes lit up like the Rafe she'd known, the boy who'd worn his heart on his sleeve, at least when he was with her.

The one she'd have sworn would love her forever. Be by her side forever.

Part of her wanted to clam up. But she was still feeling the smack of what she'd just done, asking a question just to be able to point out that he wasn't really a Colton. Didn't like the look she'd seen of herself. She would not be that bitter woman who lived alone and pushed everyone away, and then felt sorry for herself because she was alone. Not any part of that woman—except flying solo. She was okay with that. Used to that.

Knew how to do that and be happy—*and* be good to others.

"After you…weren't coming around anymore…my father told me that there was a whole world of men out there, that I didn't have to settle for being on a ranch in the middle of nowhere…"

His lips tightened. So maybe her reasoning for bringing up her mom hadn't been completely altruistic. Maybe she was still digging at him a little. But he had to know the one to understand the other. Had to know why, after all his years of silence, her father had finally opened up about the mother she barely remembered.

"That's when he told me that my mom had left him for a city man. Because he had so much more to offer her. A whole life of exciting experiences. I think he was trying to comfort me," she said. And knew that what she was really doing was telling Rafe something that she'd yearned to tell him long ago.

Something she'd needed to run to him with; only he hadn't been there.

She still wanted him to know. Not to hurt him. But just to be able to tell him.

"What I figured out, though, was that she gave up custody of her kids for the allure of bright lights."

Like Rafe had given her up for the chance at finer things. She looked over at him, having completely lost what little appetite she had.

He studied her, his blue eyes shadowed, and put down his fork. "Like I did. That's what you're thinking." She didn't say a word. "It wasn't like that, Kerry."

"How do you know? You don't know my mother."

"I didn't leave you because I wanted what the Coltons could give me."

"Sure you did. I don't blame you, Rafe. Seriously. You were five when your father died. You had no say in what happened then. And later...you were only thirteen. Where were you going to go? Who'd support you? I get it."

Right up until he'd become an adult. They'd both returned to Mustang Valley—he had to have known that he was part of the reason she'd come back—and yet he'd never contacted her.

He looked like he had more to say, lifted a hand, palm up, and then let it fall. "Anyway, you looked her up. When? Did you find her?"

"I did," she said, letting the rest go. Because there was no point in not doing so. They'd both made their choices. "I went to college at Arizona State University, in Phoenix, and during one of my criminal justice classes, we were doing investigations… I looked her up. It didn't take much to find her. She wasn't hiding. All I had to do, really was look up her name online…"

"So…" His gaze intent, he leaned toward her and he was that boy again, or she wished she was that girl, telling her best friend one of the most important things about her. And knowing he really cared and wanted to share it with her.

"I called her. She sounded happy to hear from me. Agreed to meet me…"

She could feel the moisture start to seep in at the sides of her eyes, but smiled, looked him straight in the eye.

"I knew the second I saw her she was an addict. She had the scabs on her face. Was skinny and sunken in. Her skin…" She shook her head. "All she wanted from me was money to feed her habit."

Head shaking, Rafe reached for her hand. "I'm so sorry, Ker. So, so sorry. It's so incredible that you've managed to make such a great life for yourself, in spite of having both parents as addicts."

She shook her head, too, and took her hand back, using it to feed herself another bite she didn't want. She didn't want his admiration. She wanted him to know her well enough to just assume that of course she would have made something of herself. "I tried to help her," she said. "Got her into rehab, gave her what little money I had." Then she shrugged. "But you know how that goes. I finally had to admit that I was nothing to her, not emotionally. I meant no more to her than anyone else from whom she might get a handout. She was prostituting herself for drugs the last time I saw her. She'd been making her choices her whole life and I wasn't going to change them."

"Did you tell your dad?"

"No." What point would there have been in that? He'd died never knowing what his wife had become in her effort to get away from him and his life on a ranch.

Her parents probably loved each other once. And the pain of loving had brought out the worst in both of them. Maybe her father had already been drinking too much. Or her mother had been using. All she knew was that the failed relationship had been the final nail in two coffins.

She wasn't going to let that happen to her. Wasn't going to let romantic love, partnering, matter that much to her.

Especially not with her genes. Her mother, her father, brother…

"I'm not going to be like them, Rafe." She couldn't help the fear in her voice. Was pretty sure he could see it in her eyes, too.

"Of course you aren't." He sat back, sounding all Colton, and completely sure of himself. "If you were, you'd have been there long ago," he added. "Look at all you've been through, and here you are, completely sober, spending your life finding justice for people you don't even know because that's who you are."

He made her sound…admirable.

Like some kind of celebrity.

And that was a dangerous road for her to get on. Because, as far as the Coltons were concerned, she was, and always would be "the help."

* * *

He slept on the couch, waking every two hours to walk down the hall and peek into Kerry's open door and make sure that she'd awoken with her alarm. It was probably overkill. He didn't care. He wasn't taking any chances.

His world without Kerry in it was one thing. The entire world without her... That was just wrong. Funny how he'd never realized that before. Had never acknowledged how good he felt, knowing that Kerry was only a few miles away from him.

Just like, as a kid, he'd liked knowing she was just a couple of acres away.

At the 3:00 a.m. alarm he was already awake. They'd gone over the aerial photos. Had a plan of search for the next day, assuming Kerry woke without a headache. She also wanted to head back to the hospital to talk to employees—find out if any of them knew of anyone who'd worked in the maternity ward forty years before. Or if they knew anything about the fire that had destroyed all of the nursery records.

He'd told her he'd already been planning to talk to people at the hospital in the hopes of finding some information on the ob-gyn who'd been working the night Ace was born, on behalf of the Colton Oil board, and she'd agreed that they could do so together. Payne's shooting had happened at the same time that the family had been reeling from the email that had outed Ace Colton. The timing was too coincidental for Kerry. She needed to know if the two incidents were connected somehow. They knew, from Callum and Marlowe's search that the records had all been destroyed, but that didn't mean someone wouldn't remember a doctor or nurse who'd worked there.

All the unanswered questions in his life had him awake. Making mental columns. Figuring.

Financial wizardry was easy compared to life. Numbers always followed a pattern. There were no exceptions. But all this—babies switched at birth, bodies thrown over mountains, attempted murder—just didn't compute.

How did he solve it all?

Kerry was sitting up in bed when he made it down the hall to check on her. The top half of the T-shirt she'd had on all night was visible above the covers. Even in the dark shadows he could see the unfettered mounds of her breasts. The shapes of her nipples...

She'd taken off her bra. What else had she removed?

"Let's take Odin Rogers out of the mix for a minute," she said. "It's telling that I've had two attempts on my life on that mountain, but in town, I just get a brick thrown through my window. A warning to stay off the mountain..."

He could see her frown in the darkness, moved forward to sit on the end corner of the bed. Clearly, her mind was working just fine. And keeping her awake, just like his was.

"What does that tell you?" he asked. He had his own theories, but wanted to hear hers.

"That they think I don't know anything, yet," she said. "I'm only a threat to them up on that mountain. Which means, as we thought, there's still something up there they don't want me to find. But it also tells me that the mountain is the only place they think we'll find anything. And that maybe who's doing whatever they're doing up there isn't from Mustang Valley, or hanging out here. When Dane and I talked to Rogers yesterday morning, he was almost laughing at us, he was so pleasant. He didn't care at all that we were looking at him. Because he was confident we wouldn't find anything."

"So what if Rogers isn't involved?" He had to put the thought out there, regardless of what she thought she knew. Because the possibility existed. "Could be both deaths up there, Tyler's and the rangers, had nothing to do with Rogers. Maybe your thought about guns and drugs is right, but maybe Odin isn't involved."

She shrugged. "Could be. I don't really care if it's him or not. I just want to get whoever it is."

Because she wasn't carrying a vendetta. She truly wanted justice. That's all she'd ever wanted out of life, he knew. Things to be done right. Fairly.

And when had that ever happened for her? Certainly not in her personal life. He'd suffered, as well. He'd lost her, his only true friend in the world. His deepest love. But he'd gained one hell of a lot, too.

"I'm wondering if maybe the ranger, this Grant Alvin, stumbled onto whatever it is no one wants us to find. Maybe he was afraid we'd suspect him because he hadn't notified anyone. Or maybe he wanted us out of there because he was up there trying to cash in for himself. Robbing from the robbers," she said. "That would explain why he was threatening us, but then ended up dead.

"We know Odin runs a drug gang in the county,"

she continued. "We just can't pin anything on him. I'm not sure about weapons, but with the amount of money he has, it makes sense. And if it was just drugs they were hiding up there, they could move them pretty easily. Ammunition, not so much."

When she said it like that, building a mental picture of a stockpile of explosives, he wanted her nowhere near the place.

And he knew there was nothing he could or would do to stop her. The reality was, her work was dangerous. Her life was in potential jeopardy every time she went out to question someone.

Any day could be her last.

And he was sitting on the end of her bed, wasting perfectly good hours, when he could be soaking up the essence of her.

And hopefully bringing her pleasure. Maybe even making her happy.

They'd both stopped talking about the case. Had been studying each other for a good minute.

"I want to make love with you."

She continued to stare at him.

"I'm here." He shrugged. "Who knows if I'll ever be here again? Twenty-four hours ago, we were doing it. What's one more time going to hurt?"

Maybe plenty. He had no calculator for such a thing. He also had to ask. Something was telling him she needed him as badly as he needed her.

"We've got a few more hours until dawn," he said. "Let's not waste them."

His heart dropped when she nodded and pulled back the covers.

* * *

She'd let herself down by spending the night with Rafe again. She wasn't going to make it worse by beating herself up over it. So she blamed it on emotional residue that was the result of having allowed herself to be carried by her hero down the mountain to safety.

She didn't have a hero. Didn't need one.

And would have kept herself safe up there. She'd been ready to pull her gun if she had to. Would probably have suffered worse injuries in the scuffle, might have been off her shot. Getting down the mountain in her condition would have been challenging.

But facing challenges was what she did.

Daylight saw her feeling fine, injury wise, in the shower, and ready to put sex with Rafe Colton behind her. Though, if anything, that second night of lovemaking had been better than the first. Slow and tender, they'd peaked together and then had fallen asleep with their bodies still joined.

It happened. And was done.

Now she had to get to work. It was the only choice before her.

As had happened the day before, he'd been out of bed by the time she'd fully woken. As soon as she heard him close the door to the hall bath, she'd scurried into her own ablutions. Planned to beat him to the coffeepot.

She liked her brew her way—a combination of medium and dark roast, French and Italian. She was high maintenance, so sue her. As long as she was the only one being called upon to maintain herself, there'd be no problem.

Cup in hand, half-empty already, she faced the hall as he came down it.

"No more sex," she said, looking him straight in the eye. "I only do that when I'm in a committed relationship," she told him. "The first night…well maybe we owed that to the past…but no more. We can work together. I recognize that I have a better chance of finding Tyler's killer if I have help, and I understand your need to help. Just like having you with me at the hospital gives me quicker access to whatever we might be offered, and also might help people open up to us, as it makes our questions more personal. Our minds always seemed to meld well and solve problems, even as kids, but that's it, Rafe. Don't think you're going to insinuate yourself into my investigation of Ace, to sway me in his favor. And do not ask me for sex again."

His blue-eyed gaze seemed to be pleading with her.

"If I don't say no again, I'll start to hate myself. So I'm asking you not to put me in that position."

His nod told her she'd won.

So how come she felt like such a loser?

For all the excitement they'd found on Mustang Mountain the past couple of days, that day they only ran into a couple of hikers, tourists who were on their way from Tombstone to Bisbee and were spending the night in Mustang Valley. Kerry filled them in on eating choices, spending more time selling them on Bubba's Diner than on Rafe's two preferences: Lucia's and the steak and seafood house. He didn't intervene. What did he know about being on a tourist budget?

Or about Bubba's, for that matter? He hadn't eaten there since his biological father died.

They stopped at the lay-by where Kerry had seen the car the day before. Climbed back up to where Rafe had run into the thug who'd hurt her. As the chief had said, there was no sign of anyone having been there. And no indications of human life anywhere around the trail Kerry had been on, following the guy. If there was a cave out there, it was either much farther in, a hike that would require supplies and more time than they currently had, or it was so well hidden they were walking right by it.

"Maybe the ranger's death spooked them," she said as they turned around. "Could be the guy I followed yesterday was out here on Odin's orders to move their stash. For all we know it could be safely relocated by now, on foot, after dark. It's not like there's a shortage of mountains out here."

He knew she was frustrated all over again, but he was relieved that they'd made it off the mountain without further trouble. Maybe she'd be done with the whole Odin Rogers thing for a day or two, while Dane continued to investigate Grant Alvin's murder, going over the autopsy report, doing what cops did during potential murder investigations.

Maybe she'd lie low at least until he heard back from Jason. He'd rather know his adversary before meeting the guy's goons unexpectedly in the dark. Or up on the mountain.

Kerry had insisted on driving her Jeep because she was the one carrying a badge and gun, and she didn't say a lot as they headed back through town to the hospital.

He wanted to tell her how much she meant to him. To ask her if they could try to find a way to be together sometimes, not just for sex, just to be—but knew it wouldn't be enough. Not for either of them. Most particularly her. He'd be positioning her for a life alone with only occasional visits from him to break up the monotony. And he knew that even if she said yes, she'd regret it someday. He'd regret doing it to her.

She parked in the visitor lot and turned off the ignition. He'd changed from work clothes to jeans and hiking boots before leaving his office at Colton Oil just after lunch that day. Would have liked to have changed back before heading to the hospital, but intended to walk in beside her just as he was.

Payne wouldn't approve. So this would be the day that he woke up.

Pray God, let him wake up.

As much as Rafe sometimes kept himself distant from the older man, he loved Payne. Respected him.

"You're sure you want to be seen in here with me?" Kerry asked, turning to him in the Jeep, with one foot already out on the blacktop.

In her blue tweed pants, light blue cotton oxford, and cowboy boots, and with that gun hanging from her belt, she was all business. She'd pulled her hair back into a ponytail. He had a sudden vision of that long, straight auburn halo half covering him as she sat on top of him, and shook the vision away.

He was proud of her. Of what she'd made of her life.

"Of course I want to be seen with you," he told her.

If his family saw them together, he only had to say he was making use of police resources working on the case—finding out who switched Ace at birth, and that he was trying to help Kerry find who shot Payne, so that she'd leave Ace alone. And other than the family, he didn't much care what people saw or thought.

He was the Cinderella boy. The cowboy's kid who'd been lucky enough to be adopted by the rich and famous Coltons. It didn't matter what Rafe thought or did, or who he actually might be; no one saw anything but that feel-good story. So he'd quit trying to be anything else or getting to be close friends with anyone in Mustang Valley. At home he was a bit of a loner.

When he traveled on business, he was different. He socialized. Went to the theater. Out to dinner. Lived more of a regular life.

He didn't bother explaining it all to Kerry.

Chapter 13

"Mr. Colton? The doctor hasn't been in to see your father yet today, so no news yet…" The brown-eyed blond nurse didn't even seem to see Kerry when she walked in the door of the hospital next to Rafe. "Will I see you up there?"

The woman then glanced in Kerry's direction briefly, long enough to take stock of the gun at her hip, and the badge she'd hooked to her belt loop on their way in. Long enough to dismiss her as potential competition for Rafe. She was just the cop on the case.

For a second there she thought about letting the woman know just where and how Rafe Colton had fallen asleep at four o'clock that morning, but she rose above her baser self, and said, "Have you been working here long?" Before Rafe had a chance to answer the woman's initial question.

"Ten years, why?" the woman asked, friendly enough, but looking back at Rafe as though she'd much rather be speaking with him. So would Kerry. It was the effect Rafe Colton had on women, apparently.

"I'm looking for anyone who might have worked here forty years ago. Or who knows someone who did."

The woman—Brenda, her name badge said— nodded. "You want someone who was here that day the electrical fire destroyed all the nursery records, the same day Ace Colton was born," she said. "I heard Mrs. Colton and her daughter talking about it upstairs."

What she wanted to know was who switched Ace Colton at birth, and to get there she was hoping to find the doctor who'd delivered him, but her purpose was no business of Brenda's.

"I'd really just like to speak to anyone who might know who was working at the hospital around that time."

Brenda shook her head. "I really don't know, but if you ask Terrence, downstairs in janitorial, he'll have a better idea. I didn't think of him until I was coming down for my lunch, because he's not medical personnel, but he's like a fixture around here. The guy's like, sixty. From what I hear, this was his first job. He quit school to take it to help his mom and he's been here ever since…"

The story wasn't a surprising one. Life in the mountainous desert wasn't easy. And jobs weren't plentiful, either, unless you worked a ranch. Some of their residents actually commuted the hour or so back and forth to Tucson every day just to work a decent, well-paying job with benefits.

"Thank you," she said to the woman, and headed toward the elevator before she could see Rafe smile his goodbye. He pushed the down button before she got there.

And didn't say a word about pretty, available Brenda. Which didn't stop Kerry from thinking about her. And all of the other women who'd known the pleasures of Rafe's body over the years.

He'd have had a lot of them. And not just because he was rich, but because he was gorgeous. Smart. Kind. He had a way of focusing on who he was with, making you feel special.

But she wasn't special. She was one of many. Had been one of many. There would be no more of Rafe's body in her future.

It would be best if she'd remember that.

Used to commanding attention, and having people jump to do his bidding, Rafe struggled a bit to take a back seat to Kerry as they made their way to Terrence Jones via two other hospital employees, one of whom was hospital administrator Anne Sewall. Rafe had already spoken with the woman the morning after Payne was admitted, but when she started to address him, to answer Kerry's questions about a janitor named Terrence, he took a step back and looked toward Kerry. Anne, a professional, sixtyish woman with her blond bob and wire glasses framing brown eyes, took his cue and not only gave Kerry the man's last name, but walked them down to him.

Terrence was an interesting fellow. Someone Rafe felt he'd like to have a beer with just to be able to sit and listen to his observations—that was if a Colton ever had a beer with a janitor. Terrence knew nothing about the fire, other than remembering hearing about it and calling in to make sure that they didn't need him to come in. He'd taken vacation that week to be home with his mother and younger siblings for the holiday, and had no idea what medical personnel had been working. Back then he'd been in charge of cleaning labs, not wards.

These days he ran the whole janitorial department.

"I do know someone you might want to ask, though," Terrence said, glancing from Kerry to Rafe and then back. "Noelle Lando. She's been a nurse here for about as long as I've been around. She's sixty-five now and someone was trying to get her to retire, but that ain't gonna happen. Not yet, anyways. I'm not sayin' she was in the maternity ward back then. Just that she was working here and might know who was. I think she's up on surgery now, but maybe its pediatrics. Something with the older kids."

Kerry went right back to the hospital administrator, Anne, who'd told her she'd do anything she could to help. The woman made a call and within minutes Kerry and Rafe were sitting at a table within a little conference room on the second floor with Noelle. In scrubs, and with her blond hair in a bun at the back of her head, the nurse frowned as Kerry asked about the day of the fire.

"I was working days then," she said, seated directly across from Rafe. "I remember Mrs. Colton coming in, in labor, while I was still there on Christmas Eve. That was a pretty exciting thing for us. The local oil baron's wife having her first child. Everyone was making excuses to get to that floor, to get a peek at her. There was some question about the health of the baby. It was stressed, as I recall. I remember hearing someone say Baby Colton..."

"Do you know the name of the doctor who delivered the Colton baby?" Kerry asked, almost as though to distract the older woman from trying too hard to come up with a name. So she wouldn't unwittingly block the memory?

Either way, he liked watching her work. Was impressed all over again.

His family had been trying to figure out who'd delivered Ace. With Tessa gone and Payne in a coma, none of them knew...

"I don't remember," Noelle said. "I was newer then and didn't work maternity. And the Coltons had their own doctor, not someone who was here all the time. I do know it was someone different than the doctor who delivered the next two Colton babies. I heard someone mention it when the second child was born a few years later. Something about how tense the first delivery had been and the second one being the exact opposite..."

"Do you know who was working maternity back then?" Kerry asked, when Rafe would have liked to hear more of the story. Needed to hear more of the story. Biting his tongue, he waited for Kerry to do her job.

Another frown, and a shake of the head was Noelle's response. "I know that none of them are still here," she said. "I'm the only nurse on staff who's been here that long,

"I was working when the fire happened. There was a lot of excitement that morning, I can tell you that. And not the good kind. We didn't know how fast it would spread, and everyone was running around trying to get patients to safety, directing ones who could walk by themselves, and finding enough chairs to get those who couldn't. We needed to keep the bed traffic to a minimum as much as possible because they took up more room in the hallways. The beds required use of the elevators which, technically we weren't supposed to use, but when it was a question of having a chance to get the patients out, or possibly being trapped in the elevator, we took the chance."

She shook her head again. "As it turned out, the damage was mostly in the nursery, but it could have been much worse."

"Did you ever hear how it started?"

"No. I mean, some of us talked. It was an electrical fire, so could have just been a short, but maintenance has always been a priority here. I, and some of my coworkers, thought it had been set. Which makes no sense, either. Why are you asking about it?"

Kerry looked at Rafe.

"Please just tell me about Ace's birth."

"We've always been so careful here…and with that baby…everyone was on high alert. I just can't…" She stopped again. "It was really odd how well he'd improved overnight," she told them. And then looked kind of sad. "I…um…actually… I started going back to church again, after that. It was like this Christmas miracle, you know, that he'd thrived so much in just one night… We all took turns going to the nursery to look at him!

"That's really all I know, though," she said. "We were all crazy busy that day, getting our patients re-settled after the scare and with it being Christmas Day everyone was having visitors and what celebrations they could. The cafeteria cooked a huge Christmas dinner for family, and for what patients were allowed to eat it. I managed a quick look at the Colton baby in the nursery, but like, two seconds. It was out of my way and I had patients to tend to. It was just…you know… something famous… Tessa and Payne Colton's first baby right here in our midst."

She stopped, her gaze far-off, and then stared at Kerry.

"I remember one nurse!" she said, looking at both of them. "I remember because we were all so excited about the baby, and relieved about the fire being con-tained so much more easily than expected, we were all talking about Christmas miracles and she was grousing because she'd had to stay late. She'd been on nights, Christmas Eve night to Christmas morning in the maternity ward, so the fire definitely affected her ability to leave. I can't remember her name, but it started with *N*."

Rafe glanced at Kerry, who was sitting at the head of the table and to his direct left, his own sense of at-tention on high alert, knowing she had to be getting excited, too. If they could search hospital records for female nurses whose names started with *N*, and then narrow the search to those who worked in the maternity ward…

"Nan! Her name was Nan," Noelle exclaimed, throwing her hands up off the table and then settling them back down. "Nan Belman, maybe. Telman…" She snapped her fingers. "Gelman, that's it. Nan Gelman. She was a real grump, even on normal days."

"Do know where we can find her?" Rafe wanted to jump out of his seat.

"I have no idea," the other woman said. "I'm sorry. I remember that she didn't live in town, but I don't know if I ever knew where she did live. I just remember thinking that maybe she was always such a grouch because of her commute. I know making that drive across the long desert roads into town at ten o'clock at night would have made me tense, and having to make a long drive after a shift just to get home and rest would have done it, too. A lot of people didn't like her, but I kind of felt sorry for her."

Rafe was eager to be gone, to get on with what they'd found out, but Kerry took a couple more minutes, talking with Noelle, listening to her memories. Gaining information beyond the facts, he figured out eventually. Because nothing that happened was just a series of events; it also included the motivations and feelings of the people who figured in those events. By the time they walked with Noelle to the elevator, and thanked her, he realized that Kerry had just obtained a more thorough picture of the day Ace had been switched than Marlowe and Callum had managed to do.

And it left him wondering—did she do the same

when she thought about the things that had happened to them? Did she try to put herself in his shoes—to understand the motivations and feelings that had driven him?

She wouldn't have been successful at it. There was no way she'd ever understand the boy he'd been with her, the friendship they'd shared, and put it together with the choice he'd made. Because she was missing a key fact.

Which meant she'd have spent twenty-three years spinning her wheels. Settling for solutions that didn't fit—at best. Or she was still battling the situation.

Was that why she was still single? Unwilling to trust in love? Because she didn't trust herself to know when she had it? To know it was real?

For the first time since he'd made a promise to himself at thirteen to keep his reasons for ending their friendship to himself, Rafe wondered if not telling Kerry about Payne's ultimatum had been the best choice.

Chapter 14

Finally. She was getting somewhere. She had a name. Nan Gelman. And a onetime title: maternity nurse.

If Ace Colton didn't shoot his father, and she was not at all convinced that that was the case, then there was someone else out there who could make another attempt on Payne's life. Someone from the Colton family's past? She must know something about Ace's birth, and that must be connected to the shooting.

It was just too coincidental that there had been no viable threats against Payne Colton in recent history. And then right after the board of Colton Oil received an untraceable email with the truth of Ace's lack of Colton DNA, Payne got shot? The two incidents had to be related. It was the only thing that made sense.

Could this nurse, Nan Gelman, be involved somehow? If she had information, she wouldn't want to upset the Coltons, who could sue her, but if the information helped…they'd be grateful. If nothing else, the woman would know someone else who'd worked at the hospital when she did. And surely she'd remember the birth of the first Colton child, since, as Noelle had stated, it was such a big deal to the hospital.

And Nan Gelman had worked later than planned Christmas morning. She'd been there at the time the babies would have been switched.

Kerry discussed her theories with Rafe on the miles-long drive from the hospital back to Colton Oil, where he'd left his truck. Or rather, gave him her rundown. She didn't stop talking long enough to allow him to get a word in. Couldn't take a chance that he was going to make things personal again. She just didn't trust herself not to respond.

Being with him all day, working with him—they'd never had this much time together in one stint in the past. Not since they were five at least and she couldn't really remember before that. After his father had died, all of their time together had been stolen moments over the hill behind the barn.

So, yeah, it was nice not to have to watch the clock every second, fearing that they wouldn't get told all that they had to tell.

Ironic that she now had the time with him, but didn't have the freedom to share all her thoughts. Their current association had to be all business. It was the relationship she was allowing herself to have with him.

The one she'd chosen.

She couldn't see him otherwise.

And she wanted to see him.

For now. It made no sense. Craving time with the man who'd broken her heart and soul was illogical. She didn't get it.

But she knew she needed to, if she was ever going to be fully whole and happy.

She had to find her life without him in it. Find the mystery that drew her to him and solve it. To dissolve it.

"There are trunks in the attic of the mansion filled with keepsakes," Rafe said as she pulled up to his truck. "Each sibling has one. I'll get up there and go through Ace's tonight…see if I can find anything from when he was born…"

She put the Jeep in Park.

"Can you do that? Without his permission?" It wasn't like she had a warrant. And Ace Colton wasn't likely to let her paw through his stuff. But that Rafe would do that… For her…

"He'll give his permission," Rafe said. "But yes, I can. The board has voted to actively search for who switched Ace at birth, to find the biological Colton, by any means available to us. Those trunks are accessible to all of us…"

Us. The word hit her hard. As did the fact that she'd just done what she'd promised herself she wouldn't do. She'd taken hope, for a second there, that Rafe was choosing to help her at the risk of alienating another Colton.

"Do you have a trunk, too?" She heard the hint of emotion in her voice, the lack of professionalism in the question, wished she could take it back as she looked at him, waiting for his answer.

"I do." The blue in those eyes darkened, as though he was pleading with her. But for what? He had it all.

"Okay, well…" She didn't look away. She did push her personal feelings aside. "Things to look for… A baby book, or the hospital bracelet he'd had on…some mothers save those, hers and the baby's, and they could have doctor's names on them. They used to, sometimes, before the digital age. Baby books also typically have a line to name the delivery doctor…"

"Kerry…"

She shook her head. "I'm heading in to see if the autopsy report is back on Grant Alvin. If we can establish the ranger's cause of death as a homicide, I think I can get an order to have Tyler's body exhumed and reexamined. The way they both were lying…the similarities in landing…can't be a coincidence. It has to have something to do with how they went over the side. Like, the same guy pushing them both in the same way…"

She was rambling but stopped. He didn't need to know that she'd be spending her evening at home, on her law enforcement databases, searching for Nan Gelman. That wasn't pertinent to their association. "Please keep me posted," she said, putting the still-running Jeep back in Drive.

Rafe got the hint. She read the resignation in the long look he gave her. Saying he'd call her if he found anything in the trunk, he told her to take care and vacated her space.

She told herself it didn't hurt.

* * *

Colton Oil finance business kept Rafe at the office longer than he'd have liked. As eager as he was to get up in the attic and go through Ace's trunk to see if he could find anything that would help with discovering who'd switched his adopted brother at birth, Rafe was more driven to having a reason to call Kerry. The completed trunk search would offer that.

It was like he had to be in constant contact with her.

He also had to spend time at the hospital with Payne. He'd changed back into dress pants and shirt and tie upon arrival at the office and was wearing the same as he walked into the hospital room. Genevieve was there, but welcomed a chance to have dinner with Marlowe, Bowie and Callum, Marlowe's fraternal twin, and after she left, Rafe ended up sitting with Ace for an hour, watching Payne lying unconscious.

Marlowe and Callum were going to be heading up to the hospital after dinner and then Genevieve would take the night shift.

Rafe told Ace about wanting to go through his trunk.

"Fine," Ace said, throwing up his hand. "It's not like I have much say in anything these days."

Rafe understood the other man's frustration. Probably more than Ace knew.

"You want to be there?" he asked. "We could do it tonight, when we're done here."

Ace's headshake wasn't a total surprise. Who'd want to go look through childhood memorabilia right after finding out that his childhood had been based on a lie?

At least Rafe had always known who he was, where he came from.

"I'm staying at the condo," Ace said, referring to his loft in the industrial section of town. "I saw a reporter lurking around at the mansion yesterday and I'm not dealing with that," Ace continued.

Rafe didn't blame him.

They talked about Colton Oil business for a minute or two, mostly awkward conversation since Ace was no longer on the board and privy to the confidential board minutes, which were taking up a lot of Rafe's office time at the moment. A lot of people outside of Mustang Valley and even Arizona lived off the success of Colton Oil.

Rafe turned to study the monitors hooked up to Payne. The rise and fall of every heartbeat was designated with a green line in teepee-shaped formations. The oxygen levels and blood pressure readings turned up on the same screen. He'd asked enough questions that first day to know normal ranges for all of Payne's vital statistics and was glad to see them all completely on track. That had to be good.

"I get it now," Ace said, elbows on his knees, his hands clasped, as he glanced between Payne and Rafe.

"Get what?"

"How it must have felt…you moving in with us… there, not really one of us, but one of us…"

Uncomfortable, unsure where Ace was going, and pretty sure he didn't want to tag along, Rafe said, "What you're getting at is how hard it was, not having a say in how my life was going to go," he told the other man. *That* he could talk about.

He was still paying the price for having to do what a Colton would do, rather than following his own dictates.

Ace looked at him. Nodded. And shut up.

Rafe left soon after that, not wanting to be there when everyone got back from dinner. He'd be forced to stay longer and visit. Callum, an elite bodyguard, wasn't home much, so he had a lot of catching up to do. Rafe had to get home and uncover whatever of Ace's past was stashed away in the attic.

Thinking about his plans, he kept a light foot on the gas pedal as he made his way down Mustang Boulevard, noting Kerry's Jeep still parked outside the police station, and then sped out of town. There'd be food for dinner in the kitchen at the mansion. He could grab something and take it upstairs with him.

And hopefully have an answer for the beautiful detective before too much longer. Thinking of giving Kerry answers, he pushed the hands-free calling button on his steering wheel, and asked to call Jason. So far all the man had to report was that Odin Rogers was surface clean. Just as Kerry had said, there was nothing jumping out that would enable authorities even to bring him in for questioning.

"I'm not saying he's clean," Jason told him. "Only that he's not making it easy for anyone to find anything on him. From what I can see, his money comes from investments, but I haven't been able to trace the source of the capital. It's all run through several accounts, at least one of them offshore, which doesn't necessarily make it illegal. It just makes it harder to tell."

Investments, anything to do with money, were

Rafe's forte and he passed several miles' worth of dark, deserted roadway discussing the various accounts, trying to decipher what he was being told. He ended up asking Jason to forward all of the documents to him. Since the information hadn't been obtained with a warrant, it probably wouldn't be admissible in court or actionable in terms of Kerry's investigation, but it could lead them to something separate and apart from the money laundering he suspected was going on. Like Jason had always said, follow the money trails and eventually you find the truth.

He'd noticed headlights coming up behind him as he was finishing his call, maybe even one of the siblings heading home. It wasn't like they all checked in with each other. He hadn't noticed how fast the vehicle was traveling or he might not have hung up. It gained at least a quarter of a mile on him in the time it took him to glance down at the end call button, check the road in front of him, and then glance in his rearview mirror.

The vehicle, an old four-wheel drive SUV from before they were officially called that, wasn't carrying any Coltons, of that he was sure. The beat-up front bumper, and primer on the front hood told him that much. And the speed at which the guy was traveling... Rafe watched closely, looking for signs of swerving or other erratic behavior. Was the driver drunk?

When he saw the guy maintaining control of his vehicle, he slowed down, figuring he'd let him pass. And then, once he could get a license plate number, which was only required on backs of cars in Arizona, he'd call state patrol and report him.

The plan was still in the forming stages as the grayish vehicle caught up to him. Rafe moved as much to the side of the road as he could, flirting with the shoulder, to give the other driver as much room as possible to pass. But rather than going by him, the guy seemed to bear down on him like he was going to hit him. Both hands on the wheel, Rafe quickly floored the gas pedal and got his truck back on the road. The other vehicle kept up with him, moving over to the opposite lane as though to pass, but then coming back over heading for a sideswipe of Rafe's truck. Swerving to the shoulder, Rafe kept his truck steady, bumping along on gravel and hard dirt; he drove along the side of the lane, watching the other vehicle as much as the land in front of him. Half a mile up ahead a sign loomed. He was headed straight for it.

He had no choice but to slam on his brakes. And then, swerving, he drove back onto the road, heading in the opposite direction. Flooring the pedal again, he continued on toward town. Suddenly hearing a loud crack, he was not sure what had happened. The sound came one more time. He glanced in the rearview mirror, looking to see if the old, beat-up vehicle had turned and was still on him and noticed instead that the guy's taillights were speeding off into the distance.

Heart pounding in his chest, he saw the flash just outside the driver's side window. And heard one more crack.

That's when he figured out that he'd just been fired upon.

Chapter 15

Kerry was waiting outside in the parking lot of the police department when Rafe pulled up. The second he'd called, she had a patrol car heading out to escort him in, and state police were looking for the vehicle he'd described in great detail.

When she caught herself practically running to open his truck door for him, she slowed down. Focused on the job. And stood there waiting for him to step down out of the truck.

Yeah, she looked him over carefully, noting everything from the good, healthy color of his skin, to the slightly frenetic energy about him. His hair wasn't mussed and the knot on his tie was neatly in place.

He'd changed back into business clothes after she'd left him that afternoon. Why that mattered she didn't know, but there it was. She'd been expecting him in the jeans she'd left him in.

"You're okay?" she asked, when she'd determined for herself that he'd been telling her the truth. He wasn't hurt.

"I am. I'm not so sure about my truck." He was walking toward the tailgate and she followed him.

Damn. He was right. Someone had shot at him. "There are three distinct bullet holes," she said, shaking all over again. She went down on her haunches, studying the marks, but didn't think there was any trace evidence in them. Still, "I'll get someone out here to check this," she said. And then looked up at Lizzie and James, the two officers who'd seen Rafe in safely. "Head out there and see if you can find any casings," she said, naming the approximate mile markers that should be their starting and stopping points. "I'm afraid that if we wait until morning, traffic will have ruined our chances of finding them."

And then, hoping she had her emotions in check, she looked up at Rafe again. "Dane's here," she told him, "waiting to speak with you."

His nod was appropriate. The warm, sweet look in his gaze was not.

"I'm fine, Ker."

She nodded, and led him inside.

Kerry listened with a sense of pride as Rafe described to Dane, in clear detail, exactly what he'd told her on the phone. There was nothing duplicitous about the man. His stories never changed.

His reliability had been one of the things she'd loved

about him. Rafe Kay had been the one aspect of her life she could count on.

"I didn't get a good look at the guy," he said. "But it could have been the same guy up on the mountain, without the beard. I hit him pretty hard. If it is the same man, he'll have bruises. This guy was broad shouldered, too. Dark hair, from what I could tell. And unless someone was lying down in the vehicle, he was alone."

"Are you sure enough to risk your life on that?" Dane asked.

Frowning, Rafe shook his head. "Absolutely not."

The lines on Dane's slightly weathered face deepened with concern as he looked from one to the other of them at the round table they were sharing. "I think it's clear that you and Kerry are both much safer in town," he said, but talking mostly to Rafe, who looked as put together as always, like no matter what happened to him, he just took it and moved on. Not even his tie was askew.

Dane was wearing a tie, too, but his knots were always loose, leaving room for an open top button. "I want you under protection, at least for tonight," he said to Rafe. "Here in town, if at all possible. You tell me where you'll be and I'll send a car."

Rafe shook his head. He was a free man. He'd done nothing wrong. He had a choice. And…

"He can stay at my place," Kerry blurted. "He's already been with me the past two nights…"

She'd promised herself when he left her home that morning he wouldn't step back inside, but that was before someone had tried to shoot him.

Not them. *Him.* Not up on the mountain. But on his way home. It was getting personal.

"I don't know, Kerry," Dane said. "If he's going to bunk with someone, James might be better…"

"Why, because he's a guy and I'm a woman?" she asked, quick to anger. Quick to everything these days, apparently. "Like no one ever has guys sitting in a safe house guarding women in jeopardy?"

"Excuse me," Rafe interrupted. "I'm sitting right here. I think I can decide what protection I need and how to keep myself safe."

Right. Her point to begin with. Before she'd gone and tried to control the situation. He was the one in charge of his welfare.

"I agree with Dane. You need the protection, Rafe," she said before he could refuse, before her feelings could be hurt that it seemed like he didn't want to be at her house as badly as she wanted him there. "At this point we have no idea what's going on. Until now, the only real danger has been when we've been up on the mountain. This…following you out of town, or worse, sitting in wait for you to head out to the ranch…we can't be sure this is even related to Tyler's death, Odin Rogers, any of it. For all we know, it could have something to do with whoever shot Payne. You really need to stay in town. And you need protection."

"I can pay for my own protection," he said, and she let out a breath, glad to know he wasn't arguing his need for it. And hurt that he didn't want her services.

Hurt, because she was a confused mess where he was concerned.

And then she remembered. "You already told me

once that you'd hire your own protection," she said. "If you did, they've failed miserably…"

"I didn't. But I will."

"Now? Tonight?" Why was she fighting so hard to have him at her house? She knew what would happen. And knew that she was only creating more heartache for the future.

"Probably," he said, bowed his head and then glanced at both of them. "I'd rather wait until morning," he said. "I have a guy who has people on call, but I just told him this morning I didn't need anyone. And I'm hoping by morning we'll realize it's not necessary. None of my other siblings have watchdogs on them at the moment."

"None of your other siblings have been warned away or shot at recently. But you're right, we'll probably know more in the morning," Dane allowed. They had the ranger's autopsy results. His death had been ruled a homicide. There'd been very clear pressure applied to his throat at or about the time of death, pressure, not a blunt force blow sustained in a fall. But enough to render him incapable of calling out or fighting much if he was being backed up to a mountain ledge. These were all things she had to tell Rafe.

Because he was helping her investigate Tyler's death.

Because her brother had most likely suffered the same fate.

"We got a partial fingerprint that we've sent for identification and to be run through databases," was all Dane said about it.

If they knew who'd pushed the ranger, they could

bring him in. And maybe it could all just be over if the print came back belonging to Odin Rogers. Or whoever it came back to rolled on Odin Rogers. Or if the criminal was just plain guilty and Odin was no more than the greasy snake many of them thought him to be.

"And they might find the guy who took a shot at you. There aren't that many ways off that road, and the state police know the area. If nothing else, we might get something on the bullets that will link us to the shots fired at you two on the mountain," Dane added. "So definitely, for tonight at least, it's best that you stay in town."

"I was going to say that I'd like to accept Detective Wilder's invitation to stay at her place," Rafe said, glancing at her, briefly, and then looked back at Dane. "We've been at this a few days already and it would be less awkward," he said.

"As long as you're sure you don't mind a guest for one more night?" He looked at her fully then, and there was nothing at all untoward in the glance; nothing that Dane could ever intercept or interpret in any way inappropriate.

But as she assured both men that she was just doing her job and happy to be able to help, she knew what Rafe had been asking.

And what she'd just agreed to.

He'd given his word that he wouldn't ask her to make love with him again. But if she invited him home, all bets were off.

At least that was the translation she understood.

He would have liked to go home and refill his overnight bag. Instead, he changed into the flannels and

T-shirt that were still in his duffel from the night before and gave the rest of his clothes to Kerry to throw in the wash. The pants were dry clean only and might not survive, but if they didn't they were easily replaced.

She'd barely said a word to him, other than telling him she'd do his laundry. He'd followed her home and, at her earlier instruction, parked his truck in her garage, then waited as she pulled into the driveway behind him.

He could easily have stayed at Marlowe's condo.

He could have called Ace or got a room at the Dales Inn.

He could have done a lot of things.

He did what felt right rather than what the family would have expected of him. The distinction was small. Overall no one watched over where the others slept. But somehow over the years, family expectations had become a major measure in the choices he made.

"I just got off the phone with Bubba's," Kerry said, coming in from the laundry room to join him at the dining room table. He'd insisted on a stop at Colton Oil to collect the laptop he had there. If nothing else, he had financials to study that night. "I ordered a couple of rib plates."

One of his favorite meals of all time. Even with his well-traveled palate. He glanced at her, ready to ask if she'd remembered, and then stopped. He'd given her his word that he would never again ask her to have sex with him. He was going keep that word, which meant he couldn't be taking any trips down memory lane. With or without her.

Seeming to be on par with his mental state, she

spent the next several minutes giving him the details of Grant Alvin's autopsy. "The coroner ruled his death a homicide. And since he was killed, and even lying in a position similar to Tyler, this should be enough to get Tyler's body exhumed," she said. "To have my brother's death ruled a homicide will let us open an official investigation. Not that I'm going to rock that boat at the moment, but that fingerprint Dane told you about? It's from Alvin's neck. If we get a hit, we'll know who killed him."

That was the best news he'd heard all day. He told her so and followed it quickly with, "Is there anything back on the rock that was used to hit you yesterday?"

She shook her head. "No clear prints. But if we get this guy tonight, the chief will probably get a full confession out of him. He's the best interrogator I've ever known."

He wanted to be the best she'd ever known. And was truly glad to know that she had people in her life who were far better at some things than he was. She was looking at him. They'd been talking about the case.

He had to keep his mind focused. Stop trying to make things personal.

"Did you have a chance to look up Nan Gelman?" he asked, because it was the first case detail that sprang to mind.

"I was just getting started when you called," she told him, leaving him to wonder what else she'd been working on. To be followed by a reminder to himself that it was none of his business.

Starting up her laptop, she sat down, still fully

dressed in the clothes she'd worn all day, besides the gun she'd taken off and laid on the table beside her. Her hair was still tightly secured in a ponytail. He figured that for a good thing. The last thing he needed was to have those long auburn tresses moving freely around him.

"You mind if I set up here?" he asked, pointing to a spot where, with a couple of folders moved, he could have some free space.

She grabbed the folders, showed him the closest electrical outlet, offered an extension cord and then sat down to work.

If he was lucky, he'd make it through the night just fine.

They ate dinner while they worked. Kerry directed Rafe to help himself to anything he wanted to drink, told him where to find things, and sat down with her cardboard box filled with ribs and coleslaw. Had she been alone, she'd have had a glass of wine. With Rafe there, she stuck to water.

"You done there?" His question broke the silence that had fallen over them for most of the evening. She looked up to see him pointing to her mostly empty dinner container. His, which looked as though it had practically been licked clean, was in his hand.

"Yeah, thanks," she said, handing it to him. He was standing. She was sitting. Which put the crotch of those flannel pants right in her line of vision. She closed her eyes. And then jumped up. She'd forgotten the laundry. "I'm going to put your things in the dryer," she said. And pretended to herself that she wasn't fantasizing as she pulled each piece of his laundry from the washer, one at a time, touching each one, as she tossed it into the dryer. The underwear was last. Boxer briefs. Two pairs. Not one.

He'd had on a black pair the night before. She'd just thrown a black pair in the dryer and the last item of clothing was an identical pair. Only these were blue. Obviously donned after his shower that morning. So... What was he currently wearing?

The answer was fairly obvious. Those flannels were it.

The woman inside her got a little bit excited at the thought.

Chapter 16

Kerry's phone rang just before nine. "It's Dane," she said, and he listened while she mostly just said, "okay" and "thank you." There were a few other things, a "you, too" and "yeah." The last was accompanied by a smile. He wanted to know what the other man had said that made her smile.

Like he was jealous.

Was he jealous?

Of all the men who were in Kerry's life long-term, he had no right to be jealous, but he was. And probably the women, too. It wasn't a sexual thing. He just wanted to be one of those who had the right to share her life.

The thought wasn't new. He'd had it many times as a kid. Could just be flashing back. He didn't think so.

But he took it like the man he was. He would never

do anything that would unleash the wrath of Payne, or any of the Coltons, on Kerry. She was too precious to be involved in their high-pressure—which sometimes translated into high-drama—stakes.

He wouldn't let any of them be a threat to her in any way. Keeping that promise to himself was more important than anything else.

"The state police had had no luck finding any vehicle even close to the one you described," she said, hanging up the phone. She sounded frustrated. "I just don't get how they keep disappearing into thin air. They've got to have some kind of hideout in the desert that we don't know about."

He didn't disagree. But… "The Triple R is in the opposite direction from Mustang Mountain. So are we thinking they're doing something up on the mountain and then hiding out on the other side of Mustang Valley?"

Her frown deepened. "Or the guy after you tonight didn't have anything to do with Odin Rogers, Tyler's death, or Grant Alvin's, either."

"Unless he was purposely waiting for me," he said. "You were warned to back off or Richie Rich was next," he reminded her. It didn't make sense that the night's incident had anything to do with Payne. Killing Rafe would make little difference to Colton Oil.

"It's possible that he didn't miss when he shot that gun tonight," he continued, liking where his thoughts were taking him because they were less life threatening. "He could have fired at my tailgate on purpose. Maybe the whole thing was a warning. Like the rock through your window, and the rock that hit you yesterday. He could have killed you, but he didn't. Are we really going to believe he just has that bad an aim?"

"We don't know that it's the same man." She was looking at him. Straight at him. Something she hadn't done all night.

His mood lightened considerably.

"My instincts tell me it was." For what that was worth. If they'd been talking money, he'd put his wealth on those instincts, but thugs? "We figured we don't know yet, what they don't want us to know. So they only want us to stay off the mountain. Maybe tonight he was just giving me payback for attacking him yesterday. For getting the better of him. Some kind of revenge. Letting me know who's in charge. Scaring me off."

Kerry nodded. "Kind of makes sense," she said, and he felt like he'd just been awarded an A in class.

"What are you working on?" she asked then, still looking at him while she talked. It was as though a switch had been turned on within her. Like she'd just noticed that he was there.

He didn't want to piss her off, and knew that hiring his own private investigator to look into the case she was working on might just do that. It would point out the differences in their worlds, if nothing else.

But he'd known that when he'd made the decision to call Jason. And had done so with the intention of letting her know what he found out.

"Odin Rogers's financials," he told her.

She blinked. Frowned. "I'm sorry, what?"

God, she was beautiful. Just grab-your-gut gorgeous.

"I hired someone to look into his financials," he said, meeting her gaze because it was what he did with her. "Someone who might look at things that won't be admissible in court, certainly not without a warrant, but who might be able to give us insights that we wouldn't be able to get any other way."

She nodded. Then got up and came around the table. "So what did he find?" she asked, standing right beside him, warm and… There.

"Enough to know that you were right to suspect that he's hiding something," he told her. And then, showing her different accounts, and trails that led from one to another, opening several screens at once, he finally summarized with, "There's enough here to show us that something fishy is going on, but nothing that tells us exactly what that is. I follow all of these numbers, deposits mostly, but withdrawals, too, and match them to various other accounts to see how he's moving money around, but end up at a couple of offshore accounts that lead nowhere. There's nothing that shows where the money goes from there. But it's also not sitting there."

"These are all his accounts?" she asked.

"That's not entirely clear, either. I have account numbers, not ownership papers. I can see that some are companies—I suspect probably shell companies—but this is definitely not interest payments, which show up at the same time every month, nor is it return on investment, based on amounts of withdrawals and deposits, and the number of them. There are mostly transfers, not withdrawals. He's using a network set up by someone with intimate knowledge of the world's financial systems. And a highly trained technical person, as well." He was trying to keep it simple, but nothing about what he was looking at was simple. Which didn't set well with him. "I don't think Odin Rogers is this smart," he said.

He didn't know the guy, but from what Kerry had told him, and what Jason had found thus far...

"I don't think he is, either," she said. "He's a two-bit slime that would be pushing drugs on a street corner if he lived in a big city," she said. "But I do think he's in charge around here. I've never thought he was a criminal mastermind. Just that he somehow owns a business that traffics for them. He's a middleman. They're a dime a dozen to the guys at the top. But in their areas, they *are* the top."

"I wish I could give you more," he said, turning to look up at her and finding her breasts about two inches from his nose.

He knew their scent. Their shape and softness. Their taste.

"But it would take a skilled hacker to get any further. Someone trained to do illegal things."

He would not break his word to her. He would not ask for sex.

But if she offered?

No. That answer was clear. And solid.

Because Kerry had told him that while she might not be strong enough to resist him, she'd hate herself later for not doing so.

She needed him to have her back. Had given him a chance to be her best friend again, for a moment.

He would die before he messed that up.

* * *

She was never going to look at T-shirts and flannel pants in the same way again. She'd see them on a store display and immediately think of Rafe's solid, muscular thighs. And the apex of them. It was like she was obsessed.

Taking a break from the dining room and his overwhelmingly alive presence she made a stop in her private bathroom and then changed into a T-shirt and pair of jeans. More comfortable. Not the sweats and bra-less-ness she'd have chosen were she home alone.

She debated taking her hair down, but she never did that when she was working. It got in the way, hanging over her shoulder, lying around on the computer keys and papers in front of her.

But Rafe liked it down. He'd told her so the other night. In the bed that was only feet away from where she stood. The last time they'd been together as kids, the day they'd shared their first kiss, she'd been complaining about her hair. She'd had a big knot at the base of her neck; getting out the tangles had practically made her cry. She'd told him she wanted to chop it all off.

He'd said he'd love her the same either way, and she'd pressed him for his personal opinion.

"Never cut it." She remembered his words so clearly. And the next ones, too. "It's kind of like silk and when I touch it, I…feel…things."

He'd been so young. And heartbreakingly honest.

She pulled out the band holding her hair back. Glanced in the mirror. Met her own expression, and put the band back in.

The past was past.

And maybe it was time to cut her hair.

"I was sorry to hear about your dad," Rafe said, the conversation out of the blue, as she walked back into the dining room.

She'd spent the last several minutes living in the past. How did he know that? He couldn't possibly know that. Which meant he was there, too.

Was she wrong to deny what was so clearly calling out to both of them?

But to what end?

Yeah, they'd been kids. First loves were potent. And it hadn't ended of their own accord. Not really. But it hadn't been strong enough to bring Rafe back to her once they were adults.

She kept getting stuck there.

And every instinct she had told her it was for good reason.

"I was in grad school," he said when she crossed over to her chair and sat back down. "I would have been back for his funeral, but…"

"There was no reason for a Colton heir to attend a ranch hand's funeral," she said, and was surprised at the lack of bitterness in her tone. Maybe this time with him, as hard as it was, loving him but not able to open her heart and live the love, really was helping her put the past to rest. To get over the pain and move on.

He eyed her for a moment, and she could tell the exact second he let whatever he'd been feeling go. He pointed to some printed copies of aerial photos of Mustang Mountain. "I was just thinking…there are mines in these mountains," he said. "We've got abandoned mineshafts all over the desert. There was an item recently in the news about that cross-country runner who fell in one…"

And her father had fallen to his death in one. Of course, he'd been drunk and out at night, but…

Rafe wasn't focusing on their danger at the moment…

"You think the weapons, or drugs, or whatever we aren't meant to find are in one of these," she said.

"I'm saying it's something we haven't considered. Maybe they're using more than one. There were hundreds of guys out here in the gold rush days, covering these mountains and the desert. Think about it…we're looking for caves, aboveground structures, because there's no digging going on, no indication of fresh ground breaking, but what if the opening is overgrown with tall, dense vegetation? What if Odin just happened to be messing around up there when he was just a two-bit punk, not a rich two-bit punk, and he stumbled upon one of these shafts, and what if he grew a business from there?"

Or someone else did. She was shaking in her seat. Literally. Staring wide-eyed at Rafe.

"That's it!" she said. And then, "Oh my God, Rafe! That's it!" She was so excited she didn't know what to do with herself. Two years of trying to figure out what she was missing and there it was. She'd been looking in the wrong place. Proof of Odin Rogers's wrongdoing wasn't *on* the mountain; it was *in* it!

Half expecting Kerry to launch herself across the table to hug him, Rafe watched the expressions cross her face and knew that in all his travels he'd never seen art as exquisite as her face in those seconds. Sappy, maybe. Also true.

And he'd provided the current supplies to the artist. There was something so humbling, and so powerful in that, a sense of success he'd never known. All the numbers he'd crunched, the investments he'd spear-headed, the deals he'd closed, and nothing had felt as great as helping Kerry reach her goal.

Not that he didn't love his work—he most definitely did. He thoroughly enjoyed fine art, too. Still, it was eye-opening to find that there were things in life he'd yet to experience. New opportunities to be had, rather than just enjoying more of the same.

She was busy riffling through Mustang Mountain photos, both aerial and otherwise, and marking the spots they were familiar with. The mesa from which Tyler had gone to his death. And the one from which the ranger had, per the autopsy, been pushed. The lay-by where she'd been hit, and the mesa above it where he'd taken the goon down.

Temporarily.

She marked the trail she'd climbed to get to where she'd been hurt. The place where the old black car had been parked.

"We can cross-reference this with what claims re-cords exist from back then," she said. "I know there were a lot of squatters, and chances are Odin's using a mine that doesn't have an official claim on it so it's not known to anyone, which makes it more valuable to whoever he moves goods for..."

She broke off, looked at him, and then said, "If it's

Odin, and if it's a mine, and if there's illegal drug or gunrunning," she said.

Rafe smiled, shook his head, "I wasn't questioning your theory," he said.

"You had a funny look on your face. Like you thought I was getting ahead of myself. Like you had doubts…"

"I'm doubting the wisdom of telling you something," he said.

Her frown was instant and he accepted the physical manifestation of her confusion, knowing he was going in, that he'd just opened a door that he wasn't about to close again.

"What?" she asked. "You know something about Odin you aren't telling me?"

The question was fair. Her lack of trust was fair. He'd hired a private investigator behind her back.

And he'd broken every promise they'd ever made each other when he followed Payne's orders and broke off all communication with her.

With no explanation.

And no attempt to ever make it right—other than the little bit he'd done for Tyler while she was away at college.

"It doesn't have anything to do with Odin," he told her. "Or murders and attempted murders or babies being switched at birth." He wanted to hold her in his arms, to be able to kiss those soft lips. The table between them was a symbol of the chasm that would allow them to see each other, but would also always hold them apart.

In the same sphere, but not together.

Chapter 17

"What's going on, Rafe?" With him, the sky was the limit. He'd blown her world to bits in the past. She didn't put anything past him.

"Whatever it is you have to say, just tell me. Wisdom is kind of moot at this point." She could handle whatever it was as long as she knew about it.

His struggle seemed to be honest. Something was really bothering him.

"I didn't just cut things off with you because Payne ordered me to do so."

Her jaw dropped. She felt it go. Couldn't pick it back up for a second or two. Her gaze studied every inch of his face, stared into his eyes, looking for some kind of port on which to land.

What was he telling her? He just hadn't loved her?

Okay, they'd been thirteen. He'd been pubescent. He could have wanted to check out other girls.

But why hadn't he just said so?

Why cut her off as though she wasn't worth anything?

Still… He hadn't loved her?

She glanced at her computer screen. Saw the latest search results for Nan Gelman. Knew she'd cared about them earlier.

Nothing in the world made sense, or mattered, if Rafe hadn't loved her.

She shook her head.

Or maybe it did. Maybe this was what she'd been missing. Was that it?

Just as he'd exposed the mineshaft idea, the one thing she'd missed, was he letting her in on a little personal detail, too?

Well, then… Okay. She'd process. Deal. Grieve. All the things she did when she was alone.

For a second there she feared she was going to cry. Right then. Right there. She could feel her throat tightening. The pressure building behind her eyes.

Then it was gone, replaced by red-hot anger. How dare he…?

She wanted to throw something at him. A big something. Right in the middle of that face that had haunted every fantasy, and played a part in every bit of lovemaking she'd ever known.

"He gave me an ultimatum," he told her.

Yeah, so—that was no reason to ruin a girl's life. To steal away her belief in her own worth.

To rip hope and dreams out of her world for a while.

Or forever. She went back and forth on that one, still staring at him. Speechless.

"If I was ever caught even in the area of the cabins, or was seen anywhere within talking distance of you, he was going to have your father fired. He knew about your dad's drinking, said he only kept him on because of my birth dad. And, I'm sure, because your dad was a great cowboy. One of the best, from what I've been told. What I know is that he wasn't kidding, Kerry. You and Tyler would have been homeless with an alcoholic father looking for work that he wouldn't have been able to find anywhere within Colton reach."

She kept her mouth closed. Felt everything within her drop. Just drop. Her shoulders, her muscles, her stomach. It took a second to comprehend what he'd said.

To picture the thirteen-year-old boy she'd known being told that an entire family's future rested on his shoulders.

And thought of what he'd told her about watching her head out toward their safe place. He wouldn't have been able to go there, even when she wasn't there. He'd have had to walk by the cabins to get there.

All those years… She'd gone to their spot, sat. Waited. Hoped he might show up. Believing that someday he would.

So, she guessed, he hadn't stolen the hope and dreams away right at the beginning. That had happened slowly, over time.

And for him, a young man who'd lost everything dear to him. His daddy, and then his closest friend…

He'd always told her that she was the only person in the world he fully trusted.

To have had to make that decision…

And to have done so.

He'd been a boy and had chosen like a man. Lived like a man.

The tears filled her eyes, after all, as she stared at him.

She let them fall.

He swallowed. Licked his lips. Blinked.

"Why didn't you tell me?" she asked. Payne had allowed him to tell her that he wasn't going to see her anymore. He hadn't wanted anything left between them.

In that, Payne Colton had been somewhat decent to Kerry, not leaving her wondering. Or maybe he'd just been making sure she stayed away from Rafe. She'd been back and forth on that over the years.

"Because if I had, you'd have said you didn't care about the threat. You'd have been willing to lose your home so we could stay friends."

"It's a choice we should have made together."

"We were thirteen, Kerry. It wasn't like we could get jobs and support ourselves, make our own ways in the world."

"We could have come up with a plan. Some way to communicate…" She'd certainly come up with some crazy ideas over the years, like writing in code on a bathroom wall in a public restroom in town.

"You had to get on with your life, not hang around waiting for me."

Because he'd been getting on with his.

The reality hit her.

He'd loved her with his whole heart.

She'd been his world.

He'd have stayed with her forever if he could have. Would probably even have married her, like they used to talk about when they were eight and had no idea what marriage really meant, except getting to live in the same house.

And if they'd been able to continue being friends, they probably would have had their happily-ever-after.

When Payne had forced him to break up with her, his heart had been just as broken as hers.

But then...

He'd made a choice. And he'd moved on.

That's why he hadn't contacted her later. When they'd both returned to Mustang Valley after college.

All these years, she'd hung on to who they'd been. To him. To the love they'd shared. She'd made it sacred. Which was why the hurt couldn't leave, why she couldn't get past the pain of his betrayal. Holding the pain made the love she'd known real. It had given her a way to hold on to him. And she had most definitely been holding on, living in Mustang Valley, comparing him to any other man she'd ever dated, even keeping her hair long. She'd held him in her heart.

And he'd let her go.

Rafe watched her, waiting for a reaction. Some clue that would prompt response. Kerry just sat there, like she was thinking over what he'd said, giving no indication how she felt about it all. Or him.

When she didn't engage, he wanted to raise his voice to her. Get her attention.

He needed to tell her that he'd never stopped loving her.

He started to regret telling her his secret. He'd thought it would be for her good. To let her know that he hadn't just abandoned her because she wasn't worth enough to fight for. But that he'd loved her that much. That she'd mattered.

He was giving her the solution to the mystery that was their past.

Giving her closure.

Or had he been hoping to open a door? Or, more accurately, her heart? Was that what this was about? He'd found what he'd presented to himself as a selfless justification for letting her know that he'd sacrificed everything for her. Made it about helping her.

But was he really hoping to launch himself back into her private world? To at least gain her trust back again?

Because if that was it, he had to stop.

He had no more to offer her sitting at that table than he'd had twenty-three years before. Time had passed, but his choices would be the same.

And this was why he didn't do relationships. There were no definitive rights and wrongs. Things were too complicated in an unsolvable way.

"The only Gelman I've been able to find in census records from forty years ago lived in Mountain Valley." Kerry finally spoke up.

Rafe did a double take. Was she seriously talking about the case?

She was looking at her computer screen. "That Gelman was male, listed as head of household with a wife, but no name listed for her. They had no children. He was single when he died. There was no next of kin. There's no Gelman, Nan or otherwise, coming up anywhere else, on any databases. And none listed in hospital employment records."

Not good news. And not what he wanted to talk about at the moment, either.

"So I'm thinking…either Noelle remembered her name incorrectly…or the crabby nurse could be the person we're looking for. A woman who's capable of stealing a baby could probably have found a way to lie about her credentials, too. Maybe she got the job at the hospital, specifically in the maternity ward, because she planned to steal a baby all along. Could be it was part of a racket. Maybe they were trafficking them. Selling them to couples who couldn't have kids. It wasn't like records were computerized back then."

He listened. Agreed that her theory had merit.

"Kerry…"

"Yeah?" Her gaze was still on the screen in front of her.

"We need to talk."

That got him a glance. "We are talking."

"About what I just told you."

"No, we don't."

In all the different ways he'd figured this scenario could play out, and he'd imagined many of them over the years, her reaction wasn't even coming close. To any of them. The really good ones. Or the really bad.

"I loved you," he told her, just to make that point very clear.

She glanced up again. Nodded. "I loved you, too."

"I would never have abandoned you if Payne hadn't given me no choice. How could I love you and then get your father fired and make you lose the only home you'd ever known? You and Tyler could have ended up in foster care. They might have split you up. And your dad…he'd have drunk himself to death without the two of you. Without his work."

"He kind of did drink himself to death," she said. She was looking him right in the eye. There was no storm in her gaze, no struggle. He didn't get it.

"I did the right thing."

"I agree."

He frowned. "Then…"

"Then let's get to work," she said. "The past is past. You laid the last piece of it to rest, and I'm grateful for that. But right now we've got work to do. Two different cases to solve. Or, at least, I do. You're free to go anytime you like."

So she no longer cared if he went out and got himself killed that night?

"After tomorrow morning, of course," she said. "I'd appreciate if you'd stay put tonight. I'd have to get the chief out of bed if you left, and he'd have to find someone to protect you until morning…"

This was asinine. They go from at least caring about one another to… Strangers? Because he'd protected her family all those years ago?

She was watching him. And he saw it the second it happened, the break in her control. Saw a flash of something in her eyes before she turned her attention back to her computer screen.

"Kerry," he said, before she could slide away from him again. "Don't go cold on me. Please."

She shook her head, fire in her eyes as she glanced across at him. "What do you want from me, Rafe?"

He should have an answer to that. Drew a blank.

"Why did you tell me about Payne's ultimatum? What was your goal? What did you expect was going to happen?"

"I see you looking for answers, constantly needing to understand what's going on, and it felt wrong to be holding on to a piece of information that would help you understand your own past."

"You wanted to give me closure."

"Yes." Originally. And still. Though now he wasn't entirely sure what had actually prompted the words up and out of his mouth that evening.

"So... I got it." She was looking him right in the eye.

He was missing something vital. He didn't know what. So couldn't ask for it.

"And these past couple of days...the...connection we've shared...that's just...gone?"

He wouldn't believe that. Just wouldn't.

Her smile warmed him, and bothered him, too. "We'll always have a connection, Rafe," she said, her tone close, personal. "But it's based on the past, which has been over for a long time. I see that now. I will always love the boy I knew. Our time together will always be sacred to me..."

Why did he feel like she was digging a grave with every word she spoke?

"We're two people with a shared past who are momentarily thrown together, and I'm so thankful to have a chance to spend time with the man you've become, to get to know him, but it's not like we're anything more than strangers to each other now. How could we be?"

"You don't seem like the type of woman who has sex with a man she just met. Or with a man who feels like a complete stranger to her."

When her glance dropped back to her computer, he felt as though he'd scored a victory. And hated the game he was playing.

Because he wasn't playing. The realization was just there. He had no idea what he was doing. Or why.

"Can we at least be friends?" he asked, needing her back, in whatever capacity she'd agree to come back.

"Of course." Her smile was unfamiliar, seemed to be tinged with sadness. "Those kids we were…we'd never be able to live with them if we weren't."

Her words settled the storm inside him, something she'd always been able to do.

He decided to leave well enough alone after that.

Chapter 18

Kerry called it a night at ten. She told him they both needed to get some rest as they probably had another long day coming up in front of them. She knew she did.

"You have your choice of my bed, or the inflatable mattress on the floor between my bed and the wall," she told him. And then, just to be clear, "If you choose the bed, I'm taking the mattress and placing it between my bed and the door." She was on the job. Had agreed to protect him.

"I'm fine on the couch," Rafe said, without even a hint at hoping for more.

Even after all he'd said, she was still disappointed by that. It was so wild, how long it took the heart to catch up with what the mind knew.

What she needed was a good cry. A chance to let

her heart vent and rid itself of dreams gone dead. And she'd have it. Just as soon as she had some time alone.

"Which means I'll be on a mattress between the couch and the front door, which is drafty and it's January, so I'd really appreciate it if you could take the bed."

She was trying to be respectful, but commanding. As she would with anyone she'd been sworn, personally, to protect. She really just needed him to get his sweet ass the hell into bed, any bed, so she could take a few minutes to breathe.

"I'll take the mattress on the floor between your bed and the wall," he said, without a hint of complaint in his voice. Damn. The man sounded like royalty even when he'd been reduced to sleeping on an inflatable mattress. Because, after all, no matter where he slept, he was still a Colton.

A bed didn't change that.

Nor did her sleeping beside him.

She had to find a way to squelch, once and for all, the young woman inside her who kept trying to pretend that it might.

She had to pee. It was three in the morning. If she lay completely still and held her breath, she could hear Rafe breathing on the floor two feet from her bed. Her bathroom was on the other side of him. She'd have to pass him, risk waking him, to get there. If she went down to the hall bathroom, she'd have to open the bedroom door she'd closed and locked to give her warning if someone got in the house and tried to get to them. The sound of the door opening would wake him for sure.

Flushing was going to wake him up. No way could she go and just leave it there for him to find if he got up to go. She'd already instructed him to use her bathroom during the night.

Maybe she could hold it. She'd expected to spend most of the night just dozing, anyway. With Rafe so close, and her heart still needing him, how could she expect to sleep?

Then she'd gone and drifted right off, sleeping like a baby, until three. He could sleep another couple of hours, minimum. She wasn't going to be able to hold it.

In the sweats she'd changed into while he'd been in brushing his teeth, and the T-shirt she'd had on minus the bra, she slid out from under her sheet on the far side of the bed. Lifting her feet so they wouldn't make shuffling sounds on the carpet, she walked by Rafe's bare toes sticking out from the bottom of the sheet she'd wrapped around the mattress and made it into the bathroom.

Holding the handle in the turned open position, she quietly closed the door, slowly released the knob. She turned on the ventilation fan to muffle any noise as she hurried to the little toilet cubby, thinking ahead to time her flush with washing her hands.

She didn't look in the mirror. Didn't take time to do more than dry her hands and then, light and fan off, she opened the door as carefully as she'd closed it, her gaze aimed toward those feet at the bottom of the mattress.

They were still there. Same position.

She'd made it.

"Everything come out okay?" The sleepy voice seemed to boom into the room. Freezing on the spot at the bottom of her bed, Kerry didn't look at him. She'd told him once that her father, who'd been very drunk at the time, had asked her that one night when a couple of the other ranch hands were over and she'd been really embarrassed. To their credit, none of the other guys had laughed. Rafe had, though. And by the time they were done talking about it, she'd been laughing, too.

Everyone used the restroom, he told her. Even royalty. He'd joked about the number of toilets in the Colton mansion. The phrase had become kind of a joke between them. And not just about the bathroom. She'd do something embarrassing, like the time she'd tripped over her feet running to get to him so not a second of their stolen time had been wasted, and he'd scooped her up, watched her spit dirt out of her mouth and asked, "Everything come out okay?"

Why did she still remember this stuff?

Why did he?

Not answering him, she made it back to bed. Under the covers. Lying there stiffly staring at the ceiling.

"I miss you." His voice still sounded sleepy. Sexily sleepy. Was that it? He missed her body doing things with his after their last two nights together?

"I miss the way you used to trust me," came next.

"I miss that, too."

They were voices in the dark—that was all. It was okay.

"You think we'd have made it? If Payne hadn't

found out about us?" The fact that he had to ask was telling.

But… "Yeah," she answered. She wasn't as sure as she used to be, though. "Maybe." Because as strong as their love had been, Payne would still have been an issue.

Was still an issue.

She saw that now, more clearly than ever.

Rafe had made his choice.

The thought had been painful sitting at the dining room table filled with work and bright lights to distract her. In the dark, in her bed, in the middle of the night, the strangling pull of pain was almost unbearable.

Unstoppable.

But the way he'd talked that night, when she'd seen it all from his eyes, for the first time she got it. She actually understood. He'd had to make an unbearable choice and the only way he'd been able to do so was to harden his heart.

Against their love.

Tears seeped out of her eyes and down to wet her pillow. She'd known they were coming. But had expected to be alone when they did.

They arrived silently. Fell without sound.

Right up until she sniffed. And then had to reach for a tissue. Because nothing happened the way it did in books or on television. Real life was messy. Bodies had to pee. Noses ran.

And romantic love didn't always win.

"Come here." A hand appeared up on her mattress. She stared at it. She couldn't make love to him. Her heart wouldn't survive intact. But that hand—it was

Rafe's hand, beckoning her. Like it had the first time he'd held her hand as a boyfriend, not just a friend. They'd been standing on opposite sides of a jumping cholla, a desert plant known to reach toward anything close to it and stab it with its needles. She'd just told him that she didn't want to be his girlfriend and when he'd asked why, she'd said because she was afraid of how bad it would hurt if he ever left her. She purposely put that cactus between them, as though, if he tried to reach her, those needles would protect her.

He'd reached his hand out, rounding the cactus as much as he could without getting stung and told her, "Come here." He'd promised her that day that he would love her forever. No matter what.

He'd also said that he'd never leave her.

A month later, he had.

"Come here," he said again, sitting up this time.

"I can't have sex with you." He was an addiction she had to fight if she was ever going to be happy.

"I know." He moved his hand closer. "Come here."

In the dark, with her heart breaking, she needed him so badly. She reached out, took his hand, and when he tugged gently, she slowly left her bed and joined him on the mattress. He didn't say anything. There wasn't anything he could say; she got that.

He just wrapped his arms around her, spooning her loosely, and held her that way until she felt her tears stop and she drifted off to sleep.

Rafe woke up when Kerry's phone rang. He was alone on the mattress. Had slept surprisingly well for all the tension coursing through him. The ringing stopped and Kerry's voice came from the other end of the house. The bedroom door was open. By the smell of things, she'd already had her shower.

Had she slept at all?

The thought led him back to the sound of her tears the night before. They'd about done him in. Kerry had never been a crier. Not even when she fell and broke her arm and should have cried.

Not when he'd told her that he could never see her again.

But the night before, she'd cried.

Because of him.

He had to help her find her brother's killer and get out of her life. Payne's shooting—he'd look in Ace's trunk as he'd told her he'd do, and then he had to be out of it. The rest of the Colton siblings were going to have to handle this one without him. Unless something required a board vote, of course. He'd always be there for that.

The Coltons had taken in a five-year-old orphan and made him one of them. He was in the will as an heir. They'd accepted him as family, albeit one step distant from the rest of them, and the debt he owed for that would never be repaid. Beyond that, he loved his job. And until Payne had been shot and Kerry had come back into his sphere, he'd been quite satisfied with his life. Happy, even.

Kerry's voice had stopped. Meaning she was off the phone?

Pulling on the jeans she'd washed the night before, leaving on his T-shirt, and slipping sockless into the tennis shoes he'd worn the day before, he brushed his teeth, grabbed his stuff and headed out to the dining room.

"Lizzie's on her way to escort you out to the ranch," she said. "There's been no sign of the vehicle that ran you off the road—which is bad, but good in that whoever he was, he's off the road, at least. I'm thinking your theory that his aggression was meant as a warning, some kind of power control payback, could have been right. If that's the case, he's not going to jeopardize a multimillion-dollar business of running drugs or weapons or whatever, just to teach you a lesson."

He nodded. Opened his mouth to say "good morning" and probably to tell her that he didn't need an escort, but she just kept on talking.

"Dane called. The ballistics report was waiting for him when he got up half an hour ago. They actually got some trace off from the dings in your tailgate, and Lizzie and James found a bullet casing last night. They all match and the news isn't good."

In blue work pants again, a white shirt and with her gun back on her hip instead of under the pillow she didn't use, where she'd shown him she was putting it last night in case she was in a compromising position and he had to grab it, she sipped from a cup of coffee, not looking at him.

"Sorry, I just don't do well without my coffee," she said, and then continued. "The bullets came from a .460 Magnum, which is arguably the most powerful handgun made. But it's not the gun that is of interest. The bullets were armor piercing, prohibited by federal law, which is why they did the damage they did. I believe, and Dane is starting to lean toward agreeing with me, that whatever is going on up on that mountain has to be running illegal guns and/or ammunition. The ranger was either involved, or he stumbled upon the operation, and Tyler probably died because of it, too. I always thought it had to do with drugs, and it might, because Tyler wasn't into anything else, but we now have proof that there is at least one gun in our country that is shooting ammunition not legally sold here."

"Kerry…"

"I'm heading into the office as soon as Lizzie gets here. I want to follow up with Dane on everything he's doing, and then I have other work to do."

So Payne's shooting was "other work" to her now?

She could have more than one official case on her docket. There were only two full-time detectives in the Mustang Valley police department.

"I'd appreciate it if you get a chance to get up in the attic and look through that trunk, if you'll let me know what you find…"

Other work… Wait.

"You're going up Mustang Mountain to look for abandoned mines."

She wouldn't look at him.

"Kerry, you said we'd do this together." But maybe she had no choice. "Is Dane going with you?"

Silence was her only answer.

"Don't shut me out, Ker, please. Not now."

When she looked over at him, when he read in her eyes all the things she wasn't saying, he breathed a sigh of relief.

"I'll look at the trunk when I'm home showering,"

he said. "I've work to do at the office, but can be available to head up there by noon. Is that good enough?"

If it wasn't, he'd negotiate.

"I'll pick you up at Colton Oil at noon," she said.

You'd have thought she'd just told him she loved him.

Rafe went to the attic first. He passed Grayson on his way up the stairs. They nodded and moved on. Ace wasn't at the mansion. He didn't figure Marlowe was there, either. Genevieve had been staying at the hospital. And staff wouldn't be upstairs cleaning that early—best chance of getting up to the attic and out without having to see anyone.

He cared about them all. Generally, wasn't averse to conversation. But these days with Kerry—they were messing with him.

Something he'd like to sort out for himself, before the siblings got wind of anything.

Ace's trunk was a lot fuller than Rafe's. Made sense. He'd been at the mansion since birth, and had been Payne's firstborn. They'd seemingly saved everything. Booties. A huge folder of pictures. Dumping them on the attic floor, he spread them out with his palm, not stopping to look at the woman who'd been the only true mother figure in his life. Tessa Colton. He'd loved her more than she'd ever known. Even before Payne adopted him.

Second only to Kerry, back then.

He was looking for birth pictures. Hospital photos. There were none. No doctors at all. Moving through school records, an early reading award, he found out that Ace had been in Scouting. None of the others of them had had the opportunity to join in community circles. They'd been held apart. Special.

By the time he reached the bottom of the trunk, he was drained. And not at all happy with the idea of calling Kerry and telling her he had nothing. She'd be disappointed.

It seemed like that's all he ever did—disappoint her.

Not that she said so. Or would ever call him on it. But it was there in her avoided glances. And in her eyes when she looked at him sometimes, too.

So his confession the night before had obviously given her the closure he'd known he had to offer. He'd given her that.

And even that had fallen flat, somehow.

He was losing her.

Which was natural. He couldn't offer her a place at the Colton table. She'd never take it if he did.

She wasn't his to lose.

Hadn't been for far more years than she had been.

Opening one more manila envelope in the bottom of the trunk, expecting more photos, Rafe dumped out a slew of cards, all welcoming the new baby.

One was from the then governor of Arizona. A couple from US senators. Impressed, in spite of the powerful people with whom he'd dined over the years, he leafed through them. Regaining some sense of self. Being a Colton gave you access to people who changed the world, who could right societal wrongs. Being a Colton meant you had a say in some of the policies that governed and protected the American people.

People like Kerry, and all of the other first responders. People who needed money and support just to do their jobs. People like Tyler, who deserved second chances.

And like the Native Americans who'd had so much taken from them and were still keeping their culture alive. And all of those who fled horrendous living conditions and risked their lives just to stand on American soil.

So many times over the years, sitting at dinners meant to honor someone, or to broker an oil deal, he'd had the chance to weigh in on all kinds of policy decisions. And had had calls asking for his support for one bill or another. Mostly to do with programs for kids. He knew what it was like to feel alone in the world— to feel isolated, like Tyler had. He hoped he was making a difference.

Being a Colton mattered. He was making a difference in the world, just as both of his fathers had always taught him. Looking out for others, as his fathers had done.

And…was that an appointment card? For Tessa Colton. She was due to see Dr. Carl Hansen. The time was faded, as was the day, but the month and year— three months before Ace was born.

He'd found the doctor who'd likely delivered Ace.

Pulling out his phone to call Kerry, he stopped. How much better would it be if he could deliver the doctor to her? At least in person. And if he was at all local, Tucson, even, maybe they could go see him together, yet that day.

Trying to be respectful, Rafe threw things back in

the trunk as quickly as he could. There was no order to any of it, but nothing was damaged and it all fit.

And ten minutes later, back at his house, he was on the computer, looking up ob-gyn information.

After all the trouble they'd had locating anyone who'd worked at the hospital when Ace was born, finding Dr. Hansen was incredibly easy.

He had an address: an upscale, assisted living community. Not surprising. They were all over Arizona. People from all across the United States and Canada flocked to the fifty-five and older communities to enjoy active lifestyles after they retired. Many of them included assisted living units.

The general offices of the community in which Dr. Hansen lived weren't open for another half hour so he took the time to shower and shave. Rafe was already in his truck, heading to town when he made the call, intending to make an appointment to speak to Hansen anytime that day he'd see them. Finally, he had something that would please Kerry.

Some good news to share.

"I'm sorry, Mr. Colton," the stale female voice on the phone said, after Rafe had asked for the community manager, identified himself and explained why he was calling. All he needed from her was for her to get a message to the doctor to call him. He was a Colton. People always returned his calls. Always. And this was someone who not only knew the family, he'd been intimately acquainted with them, birthing their first child.

"I just need you to pass on the message," he said, taking care to remain patient as he explained himself again. He was not going to let Kerry down here.

Or the family, either. They needed to know who'd switched Ace at birth. To find out who was after them now. And why.

Selina might think they had to know who the real Ace Colton was, but as far as Rafe was concerned they already knew that. He was at his condo in Mustang Valley, feeling lost and alone.

And a good bit angry.

Justifiably so.

"I'd be happy to pass on the message," the woman finally said, after putting Rafe on hold while she made another call, he'd presumed, to the doctor. "I've just put in a call to his son, who holds his legal and medical power of attorney, and he's advised that I can tell you that his father can't help you."

"Let me talk to him," Rafe said, watching his rear-view mirror as carefully as the road in front of him. So far, his way into town was sunny and clear. "To the son. Have him call me…"

"He said he'd be happy to speak with you," the woman said. "Told me to pass on his number, but the son needs you to know that, until today, he'd had no idea that his father had had a Colton as a patient. He was just a baby forty years ago. And he authorized me to give you the sad news that Dr. Hansen can't help you, either. He suffers from Alzheimer's, Mr. Colton. Most times he doesn't even recognize his own son…"

Choking back disappointment, ashamed of himself for even feeling it when someone else was suffering so deeply, he offered his sincere condolences to Dr. Hansen's son and hung up.

Once again, he was forced to let Kerry down.

Chapter 19

By nine that morning, Kerry could no longer convince herself that she wasn't watching her phone. Rafe had said that he'd be checking the trunk in the attic before coming back into town. Lizzie had been back for an hour and a half, so she knew he'd arrived home safely. And he'd have called with the trunk news, wouldn't he? Did that mean something had happened to him? Either at the ranch or on his way back into town?

She wasn't going to do this, be this woman. She was practical. Levelheaded. She could handle whatever came her way. She was not a weak, worrying, slightly obsessive ninny who sent dozens of text messages a day or checked her phone every five seconds just in case. Just because you had a struggle didn't mean you gave in to it. Or became it.

So, yeah, she was still in love with Rafe Colton. Admitting that was the first step in getting over it. Every time she thought about lying in bed the night before, crying, it scared her. That wasn't her. And she wasn't going to lose herself now.

So, thinking, she left the station to conduct her morning interview. She'd spoken with Joanne Bates, a cleaner who'd been at Colton Oil when Payne was shot. On the night of the shooting, the woman had been so rattled she'd been barely coherent. Kerry had given her a couple of days to calm down and process and was heading out to reinterview. She had chosen to interview the woman in her own home, in the hopes that she'd be more comfortable and might remember more of that night.

On her way, she passed Colton Oil. She did not drive out of her way. She did, however, look over to see if Rafe's truck was parked in what she knew now to be his reserved spot.

It was. Thank God. Relief felt good.

And it was quickly followed by more negativity. Since he hadn't called her, either he'd failed to look in the trunk or hadn't bothered to let her know what he'd found. Either way, she had to calm down. Focus on her job, not on him. So he'd chosen not to make letting her know a priority. He had other things on his mind, as well.

The cases they were working together were her whole life. They were only a by-product of his.

He knew everyone she worked with. Had been to her office and slept in her home. He'd infiltrated her entire world, while he had a full life as CFO of Colton

Oil, a whole sphere of friends and business peers with whom to associate, none of whom she even knew. A separate life.

She'd never even seen his home. And the only reason she'd been inside Colton Oil was to visit the crime scene in Payne's office. She was almost a paid employee who'd been assigned to a job.

The help.

The reminder was pertinent. Timely.

She'd just been thrown for a loop the night before with his confession. It had done her heart a world of good to know that he hadn't just abandoned her because Payne told him to, but that he'd loved her enough to put her and her family first.

But that confession had been deadly, too. First, it had opened up her heart to him—let the love and longing she'd felt all those years out of the box she'd shoved them in.

And it had shown her the truth of their current situation. The boy who'd been forced to let her go had done just that. He'd let her go. She didn't blame him, was pretty sure that he'd never have chosen to move on. He'd done what he had to do to survive.

While she'd held on to their love and kept it a part of her, he'd grown past it into someone else.

It was done.

And hopefully now she could be, too. With a little time.

Joanne Bates, a forty-two-year-old divorcée, lived in a small, two-bedroom home in a quiet neighborhood with similar homes. They were clean, stucco look-alikes with two-car garages and front landscaping. The roads were clear of parked cars and potholes.

She opened her door before Kerry was close enough to knock.

"Come in, Detective," she said, her smile kind and her lips a bit tremulous. "I was just finishing the dishes. My kids are grown, but came over for breakfast," she said, leading the way into a small, square living room with matching blue couch and love seat. "They're worried about me."

Kerry waited until the woman sat on one end of the couch, and then took the other. Joanne's short blond hair seemed to bob as she spoke, as though she was hearing a beat in her head. She could have been nervously hiding something, but Kerry didn't think so. The woman was truly traumatized.

Which meant she'd probably witnessed more than she knew.

Kerry asked her about her kids, first, distracting her from what she feared. And then a little bit about her job at Colton Oil, to put the woman on the scene before delving into the bad stuff.

"I've been there over five years," she said. "I was a stay-at-home mom, and when my husband left... I didn't have many marketable skills. The Coltons have been really good to me. When my kids were home I could work my hours around their schedule. They offer benefits and I'm making more than I would waitressing or working a retail job."

"So tell me what you remember of that night," she said, leaning toward the woman, speaking softly. Letting her know she wasn't alone in dealing with the horror. That people cared and were working to solve the problem.

At first Joanne reiterated what she'd said the night of the shooting. She'd heard a gunshot, then footsteps and a stairwell door banging against the wall. She'd run toward the sound of the gunshot and found Payne on his back on the floor of his office.

The rocking grew worse and tears flooded her eyes as she mentioned the body. She'd never witnessed a gunshot wound firsthand and the sight of it had disarmed her, for sure. Moving closer, Kerry rubbed her back, hating that she had to ask Joanne to relive something that was clearly upsetting to her, but she had to find out who had wanted Payne dead.

"Is there anything else, anything that you might have remembered in the past couple of days, as you work through it all?" she asked, gently, while Joanne was still deeply inside the trauma.

"I can't be sure…"

"It's okay," Kerry told her, a tiny fissure of hope opening inside her. "Anything at all. You might not think it could help, but…"

"My vacuum is running and I might just be imagining it…but I don't think I am." She glanced at Kerry, hazel eyes wide. "I keep hearing a man's voice, saying one word—*Mom*—and then the *f* word, right before the shot," she said. "But how could I have heard talking over the vacuum?"

Trying not to show her excitement, to lead the witness or in any way affect the testimony, she said,

"If someone was yelling, you could have."

The woman nodded, her brow clearing a bit. "I'm

not sure, which is why I didn't call you, and I didn't even think of it that night… I just kept seeing poor Mr. Colton lying there, and all that blood…" She shuddered, and Kerry, with her hand around the woman's back, gave Joanne's shoulder a hug.

"This is good," she said. "Really good." And then: "You're sure it was a man's voice?"

"Yeah. It was definitely male. I knew Mr. Colton was in his office, but last I knew he was alone. I think I probably was struck by the fact that someone else was with him, but before I could even process it, I heard the shot and then…"

"I know," Kerry said.

Shaking her head, Joanne covered her ears with both hands. "I just keep hearing that one word, over and over," she said. "*Mom.* It makes no sense to me."

Mom? Payne had married his second wife after Tessa had died from cancer. Ace could have been carrying resentment from that all his life, and then to have his father suddenly disown him? Definitely more motive. It could be that with Ace's parentage in question, Tessa's other two children would go after their father as well, for the same reason. So Grayson and Ainsley just made it to her suspect list. Except, wait, not Ainsley. The Colton Oil attorney was female. Joanne said the voice was male. But she was definitely going to look into Grayson.

"Did you recognize the voice?" Kerry asked, getting that excited feel she got when she was on to something. Joanne had worked at Colton Oil five years. She'd have heard Ace's voice—a man who'd just found out his mother wasn't his mother, and then lost his job because of it.

"No." Joanne seemed certain about that. "I wish I did. It seems like it would all make more sense if I did. You know, like I wasn't just imagining things..."

"Trust yourself, Joanne," Kerry said, the words just coming to her as she said them. "Don't let this take away your inner strength. You were great that night. You heard something, and you ran immediately to help. Think about that. About how strong you were. And the rest, it's coming to you because it's important."

Joanne looked up, gave her a tremulous smile. Nodded.

"You've got my number," Kerry told her, standing. "You call me anytime, day or night, if you think of anything else," she said.

And as she walked out to her Jeep, she felt good. Better than she had in a while. Sometimes you teach what you most need to learn. Like Joanne, she did what she had to do. She had an inner strength that guided her and she just had to trust it.

That inner voice had led her to law enforcement and there was no doubt in her mind that she was doing what she was meant to do.

She might be "the help," but "the help" was what she wanted to be. She belonged in the trenches, living every moment to make the world a better place. A safer place.

Kerry pulled into the Colton Oil parking lot exactly at noon. She still hadn't heard from Rafe, but wasn't as hurt by that as she'd been before her visit with Joanne. Rafe was an incredibly busy man.

She was glad to have reconnected with him and to have the chance to put the past to rest. Glad to know that he'd turned out to be a decent guy. And was now going to focus on healing herself. Letting go. Living free of him.

They'd said she'd pick him up at noon and at exactly that, he came walking across the parking lot.

In jeans and cowboy boots this time, fancy, shiny-looking ones, not worn like the ones she had on. He climbed into the Jeep and for a second there it looked like he meant to lean over and kiss her. For a second there, she started to lean in to kiss him back.

She grabbed the bag on the console beside her instead. "I stopped at the convenience store and got a couple of ham and lettuce sandwiches," she said, grabbing one out and opening the cellophane container. "They were just made this morning. Help yourself."

"I just ate," he told her. "We had a client in and catered lunch…"

Of course he'd eaten. And nothing plebeian like a lunch meat sandwich.

"I've got some bad news," he told her as she was pulling out of the lot, and she braced herself.

So when he told her that he'd found the ob-gyn who'd delivered Ace, but that the man was incapable of giving them any information at all, she almost broke out in a smile. Almost. Because she was still in the adjustment stage of getting over him. Still, it was good to know that he wasn't ditching her. Yet.

"It was a long shot," she told him, "but thanks for

checking." And then, "Do you have time to make a stop before we head up the mountain?" she added, forcing herself to keep her mind on business. Not on cataloging every aspect of Rafe in her vehicle, storing up memories for the new future she was building for herself.

"I'm yours for the rest of the day," he said, and her stomach tumbled an immediate response. Or her heart did.

"What's up?" He'd reached for the second sandwich. Was already taking a bite. She took another bite of hers, too, thinking it suddenly tasted better.

"I did some checking this morning. The black car that met with Odin Rogers...it came back as having been totaled. And the vehicle you described coming after you last night—there hasn't been a sign of it, not on any security cameras in town or in Mountain Valley, either. So I'm thinking, maybe Rogers has access to a junkyard, and has his guys take vehicles from there. It's smart, really. No way to trace them, and if they do come up on a database, like the black one did, it's a dead end. No owner to question. I'd like to take a run out to the junkyard just to take a look. To see if my theory is even possible. And if we get really lucky, maybe we'll find last night's vehicle. Maybe not. But I wanted you with me because you're the only one who could identify it if it's there. At the very least we can get some pictures of what vehicles are there and see if any of them disappear. Or show up behind us..."

He was grinning at her. And her insides belly flopped again.

"What?" she asked.

"You're impressive," he told her. "And… I'm sure this is going to sound crazy, considering the fact that I was run off the road and shot at last night…but I'm enjoying this. Working with you."

She nodded. Smiled.

Turned a corner.

And reminded herself that he was a rich dude on a week-long onetime thrill ride, like guys who took dude ranch vacations. He wasn't signing on for life.

Chapter 20

"I do have some good news." Rafe was feeling better than he had all morning. About himself. About life. The ham sandwich was a decent stand-in for the dessert he'd missed in order to be ready to meet Kerry. They had a whole day together ahead of them. And he'd heard from Jason.

"What's that?" She drove, chewed and looked so beautiful he could hardly swallow for a second. Her hair was pulled back again, but he'd had those silky auburn tresses tangled around his arms just hours before.

"I heard from my private detective," he told her, glad he'd had good news to top the bad. Glad that he'd opted to wait to call her about Dr. Hansen until he'd heard from the PI, just in case. The stars were aligning. "Odin Rogers legally changed his name," he said, quite pleased with his information, because he knew who would be. "He's the one who named himself after a Norse god. Until he was eighteen, he was Burt Rogers."

"The Big B!" Kerry swerved for a brief second as she glanced at him, but quickly righted the vehicle. "Oh my God, Rafe. You know what this means..." Dropping the last couple of bites of her sandwich in the cellophane, she tossed it back into the bag.

"It means that you're probably right. That the only thing Tyler feared was Odin Rogers."

"He knew too much," she said. "Look what's been happening to us and we've just been getting close."

"I'm guessing that Grant Alvin knew too much, too," Rafe said, sobering completely as he thought about the man who'd died that week. He'd been a jerk, but that didn't mean he deserved to die.

The thought served to remind him that as good as he felt, being with Kerry, they weren't playing a game. Lives were at stake: his and hers.

They took a lot of pictures at the junkyard. But saw no sign of the vehicle that had driven him off the road the night before. Kerry still got in a couple of them, opened glove boxes, consoles, looked under the seats, and then around bumpers. After about the fifth rusted trash heap, she stood up, keys dangling in her hand. A car ready to go at a moment's notice.

"If we turn this puppy on, I bet we'll find a full tank of gas sitting in it," she said, and started up the motor.

Sure enough, the car sprang to life. She snapped a

photo, turned the car off and suggested they get the hell out of there before someone came looking.

Not unhappy to be leaving the symbol of life's failures, Rafe hurried with her back to her Jeep. Wanting to take her hand and run, like they had as kids, trying to get away from something or another. He couldn't remember what. But he bet Kerry would have.

More and more, Rafe was seeing just how good she was at her job. And at other things, too. Like being a hardworking employee. A dedicated community member. And a loyal friend for life.

Dare he hope that they'd find a way to stay in touch? To see each other now and then, as friends?

Hell, with his money he could afford to stay with her in Tucson's most luxurious resort every weekend.

Or fly to Italy for an evening of authentic pasta.

Or…

His phone rang just as she was starting the Jeep. *Marlowe.*

"I have to take this," he said, uneasy as a Colton pierced his Kerry time.

"Hey, I just got an email from Dee," Colton Oil's new CEO said, referring to Dee Walton, Payne's administrative assistant, who was keeping the flow of the office going while Payne was in the hospital. "She says she belongs to some self-help organization here in town, the Affirmation Alliance Group. You ever hear of them?"

"Nope." But then he wasn't into that kind of thing. Self-help, by the very nature of the word, meant you did it yourself, not as part of a group.

"Apparently the founder, a Micheline Anderson, is

pretty gifted at boosting morale. I guess she travels to various corporations and gives talks, including grief and healing workshops. She did wonders for the grief group Dee joined after her husband died last year. Anyway, she thinks it might be a good idea to bring Ms. Anderson in to give a talk to Colton Oil employees, you know, just to ease some of the tension from Dad's shooting. Especially since the guy is still out there. And help everyone to adjust to Ace's leaving and to me taking over the helm. It's a ton of traumatic change in such a short time…"

"You know I don't go for that kind of stuff, but if you think our employees would benefit…the funds to hire her won't be a problem, obviously. I'd make attendance on a volunteer basis only for employees, though…if you really think it's necessary." Because he did not.

But Rafe had discovered long ago that he wasn't like most people. While others seemed to take things to heart, to be emotionally stumped for a time when tragedy struck, he was more apt to take things on the chin and go about his business. It was a trait Payne admired in him.

One the Colton siblings counted on.

Something he'd always considered one of his gifts…

Kerry took a turn, and then another, going a good ten miles over the speed limit as she turned onto the road leading out of town to Mustang Mountain. Her chin was tight. Her knuckles on the steering wheel white, as she listened to Colton business.

"I think I'll back-burner it for now," Marlowe was saying. "Dee says that Micheline will come if asked, but no worries, either way. I like that she's being pro-active," Marlowe added, opening up another chain of conversation.

"I agree," Rafe said, adding nothing more, hoping Marlowe would get the hint from his formality. She knew him well enough.

"You're with someone?"

"Yes."

"Why didn't you say so? You really need to get better at communicating, Rafe. I'll talk to you later," she said, and hung up. As did he.

"That was Marlowe," he said, noting the tightness around Kerry's lips. She'd been fine until the phone call, so clearly it had upset her.

Thing was, he understood why. He just didn't know how to make things right. The day had been going so well.

"She was talking about getting someone in to talk to the staff," he said. "To help them deal with Payne's shooting and the executive changes." It wasn't confidential information. And she was the cop on the case.

He hated that he was justifying to himself what he could talk to Kerry about.

Hated that Marlowe's call had interrupted his time with her.

"Might be a good idea," Kerry said, her tone as distant as it had been that first day when he'd gone to the station to see her. More pleasant, but just as distant.

The more time they spent together, the more he realized how much he needed to keep seeing her—and the further apart they seemed to be getting.

"You think so?" he asked, interested in her opinion and wanting to keep her talking to him.

She shrugged, took one hand off the wheel to adjust her rearview mirror, which had him looking behind them. A newish-looking white SUV was coming up on them, then passed them.

"Guy's gotta be going at least twenty over the limit," Kerry said. "He's lucky I'm not in a squad car. I'd radio him in."

Because they were out of town jurisdiction at that point, so she couldn't pull him over? He was just glad they weren't being run off the road.

"I spent some time this morning going over all of the old claims that have been registered on Mustang Mountain," she said next, almost without taking a breath in between her last sentence. "I figured we might as well start there, because a compass will take us to them. And then, once we know what we're looking for, maybe we'll be able to spot others," she said. "And Dane and the chief know we're out here. They'll be keeping tabs on us, so we have to check in anytime we have service."

That was it. She was going to take care of business and ignore the rest. He got her message. Just couldn't accept it. His time was running out.

"Ker, you think, after this is over, we can stay in touch?" All morning long he'd been revisited by memories of her tears the night before. They made him ache in deep places he hadn't felt since he was a kid. Places he'd thought were a figment of a lonely child's imagination.

"I don't think that's a good idea," she said, staring

straight ahead, both hands on the wheel again. With all the gear on her belt, she looked so tough.

And sounded that way, too.

It didn't gel with the woman who'd taken his hand and climbed down into his arms the night before.

"Why not?"

She glanced at him, at the phone he still had in his hand. "You have to ask?"

The question was meant to put him off. Shut him up. Whatever. It didn't faze him.

"Yes, I do. Because, frankly, I'm finding it hard to imagine losing this again."

She sucked in her lips. Pursed them. Took a sip from the water bottle in the holder. There was one there for him, too. She never traveled in the desert without her water.

"Losing what?" Her question came just as she was turning onto Mustang Mountain Drive—such a fancy name for the one-lane, rugged road.

"Losing you."

Pulling off into the first lay-by she came to, Kerry faced him. "You don't have me, Rafe. We slept together. Maybe it was a really bad thing to do, maybe it wasn't. It's too late to do anything about that. But you do not have me."

He'd hit a sore spot. Wasn't sure how to salve the wound. "I'd like to know I can call and you'll answer. That you'll call me if you want to. That we can share a meal now and then."

"Share a meal. Where, Rafe? In my house? Because anywhere else in town, people will just talk. It's not like the mighty Colton board hangs out in our restaurants. And I'm guessing having me out to your house would be a no."

It shouldn't be. But when he hesitated, picturing that happening, he couldn't really see it, either. "My home is my own," he told her anyway. "I can entertain anyone I choose to entertain."

"So you bring women friends there?"

"No." He'd never dated anyone long enough to expose her to the Colton clan.

"I'm not going to be a woman you visit occasionally," Kerry said. He could see the pain in her eyes. The longing. And the shard of reality, too. "And you can't offer me any more than that. It would be suicide for me, Rafe."

That was the time to tell her he could offer her more. But he couldn't picture how that would look. How it would work.

He'd never felt so helpless in his life, looking at heaven and knowing he wasn't going to get there. No matter how good he was. How hard he tried. It just wasn't his to have...

He had felt that helplessness before—twenty-three years ago, sitting in Payne Colton's study.

"It's okay," Kerry said, reaching out to run her hand along the side of his face.

Comforting *him*? He'd been attempting to comfort her. To let her know that he was going to be there for her. That he wouldn't just abandon her again.

"I understand," she added, her voice soft and oh so sweet.

"Understand what?"

"You already let go, Rafe. You moved on. These

past few days…what you're feeling…it's just residue of long ago. It's not real. Not part of your life."

"You don't know that." He didn't know it.

She nodded. "Yes, I do."

Her confidence pissed him off. What the hell? She wasn't inside him. Had no idea what he was feeling. "What makes you so sure?" he asked, ready to point out the error in her ways as soon as she clued him into her thinking.

Because whatever she thought she knew, she was wrong.

"Because if you felt even half of the intensity I feel for you, you wouldn't be asking me just to stay in touch, you'd be asking me to share your life with you."

He'd known she was wrong—just not what about. He felt the intensity. It was burning through him. Eating away at him. It just didn't prompt the result she thought it should. Didn't mean it wasn't there.

"That's your version of it," he said. "Or maybe it's that what I feel is so intense it won't let me put you in the Colton line of fire," he said. And he immediately wanted to take the words back, too. The Coltons had their faults, their quirks, but they were good people. They were his family.

"Payne could make life difficult for you, Kerry. With the chief." He hated the admission. Hated that he loved a man who he believed could do that. "Not because of anything against you," he said as he told her what he should have said the night before, when he'd told her the truth about why he'd abandoned her all those years ago. "But because he's afraid I won't be loyal to the Coltons if I go back to my roots. It's like, in his mind, the only way I prove my loyalty to him, to my family, is to not look back. The only way I can be a Colton is to be a Colton. Not a Kay."

"I know." Tears pooled in her eyes, but she didn't look away. "I already figured that out," she said. "But here's the thing, Rafe… The way I feel about you… the way I felt about you then… What you didn't get back then was that I would have been happier living in a foster home in Tucson and being in touch with you than I was living on the same ranch as you and not being able to see or talk to you."

Emotion tightened his throat. He had no comeback. He had nothing.

He'd told her that he'd taken comfort from having her close all those years. Apparently he'd taken that comfort at her expense. Guilt ate at him. Topped with regret that couldn't be assuaged. He couldn't go back. Couldn't change any of it.

"I wouldn't have sacrificed my father or Tyler that way, but if you'd have given me the choice, I'd have tried to get Dad to change jobs. Hell, I'd have been out there looking for a job for him. I might not have found one, but I'd have tried, Rafe. I'd have shared the problem with you, let you try to think of something. But you…you'd slowly been becoming one of them… All those years of living with them, seeing me on the sly…it worked for you in some convoluted way. By the time Payne caught us, you'd already converted. You were his more than mine. You didn't even tell me what he'd said. Didn't give us a chance to find a way to be together. I'd at least have tried, Rafe…"

And he hadn't. That's what she was telling him.

And that's why she'd meant it when she said that, after the case was solved, she didn't plan to see him again.

"You moved on, Rafe," she told him. "You accepted what came at you and you became one of them and the thought of being a Colton makes me shudder. You and I...we aren't alike anymore. We want different things. We like different things. We value different things. You were smart enough to figure this all out when we were thirteen. You were right to move on. Now I have to, too."

He wanted to tell her she didn't have to. That he'd find a solution, just like she said, but he wasn't sure he would. Or could. He couldn't just walk away from the Coltons. That would be as wrong as walking away from her.

Chapter 21

Of the five mines they found that afternoon, only two of them were still viable. They were overgrown, but if they'd stepped on them, they could have gone in. One wasn't deep. Maybe ten feet. Straight down. The other was deeper, but the circumference had closed in over the years. No way a grown man would fit down it, let alone a grown man carrying contraband.

Searching was going to take time. Kerry planned to take whatever time was required; if she had to search for the next year, one acre of ground at a time, she'd do so to avenge her brother's death. Tyler, her father, they were the only family she was ever likely to have—unless by some miracle she met some great guy after she got over Rafe, fell in love and lived happily ever after.

It was the stuff dreams were made of. She wanted

to learn how to dream again. And maybe letting go of an old dream—as painful as it was—was the only way to find new ones.

She wanted to have dinner with Rafe, too, when he offered as they got back to town, but she didn't. Telling him she still had work to do at the station, she dropped him off at his truck and drove away before he'd taken more than a step or two.

Dane was still at the station and she filled him in on what she'd found at the junkyard, uploading the pictures and sending them to him and the chief. It was going to be on the MVPD radar, starting immediately. Every squad car, every officer, would keep a watch on it. They were closing in on Odin Rogers. It was only a matter of time.

"I gotta hand it to you, Kerry," Dane said, his brows raised, giving his craggy face a handsome appeal. "You're one hell of a detective. I'm sorry I didn't listen to you two years ago..."

A week ago, that apology would have lit up her world. That night she shrugged. "I could just as easily have been wrong," she told him. But she was always going to go with her instincts.

And she was always going to fight for where they led her.

Lizzie and James came in just as she was getting ready to leave, and Lizzie asked her to head over to the bar for a beer. It was the last thing she wanted—to be in public, to be with anyone who knew her and to drink a beer, which was exactly why she accepted. Growing up with her father's drinking, and later, dealing with Tyler's drug abuse, she'd always gone light on imbibing, but she could take down a couple of beers without going over her blood alcohol limit to still operate vehicles legally. She'd had herself tested, while she drank, just to be sure.

When Lizzie suggested they get a booth, and dinner, she was glad that she'd came. And after an hour of her friend's company, she was more than glad.

Lizzie had to notice she wasn't her usual carefree self. Kerry wasn't cracking jokes or complaining about Dane's superiority complex. She didn't tell her friend about the older detective's apology. Nor did Lizzie pry. She knew Kerry had been spending time with Rafe Colton. Though she knew nothing of their history, the fact that he had spent the night at Kerry's house— three nights in a row—was worth discussion. Lizzie was friend enough to leave it alone.

But as they were paying their bill, getting ready to leave, Lizzie, still in her dark blue uniform and black shoes, looked across at her. "You okay?"

She might have crumbled. The night before. Yesterday. But not anymore. "No. But I'm going to be," she said, because she was who she was. The woman who handled what came to her. And went on to have a purpose and make life better.

As soon as she pulled into her drive, walked in her door, she knew why she'd gone out with Lizzie. She'd been putting off the inevitable. The sense of loss. Of excruciating loneliness. He'd only been there with her three nights and yet it was like he owned the place.

Because home was where the heart was and he owned her heart.

For the moment.

Just for the moment. She was in the process of reclaiming it. Taking her life back.

So thinking, she drew a hot bubble bath. Lit candles. Found an instrumental channel she could stream, set her Bluetooth speaker on the bathroom counter.

And soaked while she cried her heart out.

Rafe was ready to head out. Nine o'clock was late enough that by the time he got to his house, went through the mail, checked to make certain that nothing had spoiled in the refrigerator the past few days and had a shower, it would be late enough for him to lie in bed and watch television with a hope of drifting off.

He hadn't had all that much sleep the past three nights. But suspected he'd been more rested than he was going to be in the morning. After three nights with Kerry, his own bed, even for all its luxurious comforts, wasn't calling to him.

Neither was filling out his weekly household chores list, but it had to be done. He'd had a reminder email from the staff at the mansion who took care of such things. They'd empty his refrigerator, too, when they cleaned, except that he'd specifically asked them not to do so. Quirky, he knew, but he wanted to be in charge of his own refrigerator. A throwback to the days of being a Kay and being allowed to just walk up and get food whenever he wanted. Growing up at the mansion, he hadn't been allowed to hang out in the kitchen. Funny how some things stuck with you.

He was just finishing his very short list—having been gone so much—when the cleaning woman passed by his opened door for the third time.

Waiting on him to vacate so she could finish and go home?

"You can come in," he called out to her. "I'm done here." As he spoke he sent a text to Callum, letting him know he was ready to head out. Kerry had been insistent when she'd dropped him off that evening that someone escort him home. Still in her Jeep, he called his ex-SEAL younger brother to arrange the details. Callum, who was spending most of his time at the hospital with his mother, had accepted the request without question. Rafe knew Callum was getting antsy, hanging out with them in little Mustang Valley when his days generally involved traveling all over the world to protect princesses and dignitaries.

Maybe if Callum had been home, protecting his own, his father wouldn't have been shot.

The thought came from out of the blue. And was immediately rejected as grossly unfair. Rafe admired the hell out of Callum.

Hard to believe that less than a week ago Payne had been the one working late in the Colton Oil executive offices and had been shot. An entire lifetime had passed in the days in between.

The cleaning lady, he didn't know her name, had dusted his end tables, the bookshelves, and was bringing in her vacuum.

"Were you working the night of the shooting?" he asked. A Colton Oil cleaner had found Payne.

She nodded, adjusted her vacuum cord. Stepped on the machine to release the handle for easy maneuvering.

Hands in his pockets, Rafe moved closer. He couldn't go to the woman's home, try to get a testimony from her—that would be tampering—but he could speak to an employee at work.

"Do you know the woman who found him?" he asked—even then, not able to say the words "my father."

The woman's nod was jerky. She glanced at him and away.

"But she had no idea who the shooter was…right?" He had no business asking. Just needed to know…

She shook her head. "Like Joanne told the detective this morning, she has no idea who it was…"

"She spoke to a detective this morning?" he asked, more alert as he heard the unexpected news.

"Yes. Detective Wilder. She came to Joanne's house. She told her everything, Mr. Colton. We'll both help in any way we can…"

Quickly assuring the woman that he had no doubt about her motives, he grabbed his keys and went down to wait for Callum.

Kerry had interviewed the cleaning lady that day and hadn't even mentioned it to him. Not that she had to. But he wasn't a suspect. The members of his family were the victims. She could have kept him apprised.

She was pulling away from him. He already knew that. This was further proof of it and hurt more than he would have expected. More than it should have.

"Hey, Rafe!" Callum had walked in and he hadn't even noticed. "I'll walk you to your truck and then follow you home," he said, sounding like a boss man himself. "I'll be staying close and we'll stay on a call the entire time, since we don't have radios. If I see anything, I'll alert you, tell you what to do. Your job is to do it. No questions asked. Got it?"

He grinned. Remembering when Callum was about four and had come to him with jelly all over his face and shirt and begged Rafe to help him make it gone so he didn't get in trouble.

"Got it," he said. "And this is all overkill, you know."

"Not from what I understand, it's not," Callum said. "I had a talk with Detective Wilder earlier this evening. She called up to the hospital before she left work to check on Dad. You've had at least two attempts on your life, Rafe, and that's nothing to shrug off."

Maybe not. He figured if someone really wanted him dead, he would be.

And that maybe Callum just needed something to do.

"It's nice having you around," he said, as the two of them approached his truck in the dark.

"I'm turning down assignments left and right," the broad-shouldered man said with a shrug. "There's a shooter out here somewhere and who knows when he'll be back to try to finish the job. Especially if Dad can reveal his identity, and I'm fairly certain he can, since the asshole faced him point-blank, shot him at close range. Things are quiet now, with Dad in a coma. And he's not ever left alone. Why risk getting caught killing a man if he might never regain consciousness? But if he comes out of it…"

"You're a good son." Rafe tapped Callum on the back. "I pity the man if he tries a second time." He wasn't kidding.

"You're a good son, too, Rafe," Callum said, suddenly serious, standing by Rafe's truck door, preventing him from getting in. "You and Ace, you're more like Dad than any of us. You two are the sons he wanted. Asher keeps the ranch running, but the ranch is more hobby to Dad than anything. Colton Oil is his lifeblood. Grayson, he's off saving lives instead of joining the business, and me, I'm really off, doing nothing for the family. But you and Ace…"

"I'm just doing what I'm good at," Rafe said. "Same as you."

But as he got in his truck, and felt Callum's support at his back all the way home, he actually felt like a real Colton.

And the feeling was good.

The knock at her door had Kerry pulling the gun out of her holster and pointing as she approached her front door from a little to the side of it, in case someone put a bullet through it, hoping to hit her as she answered. At six in the morning, she knew that whoever was there wasn't making a common house call.

She caught a glimpse of the street in front of her house, looking past the front door through the window in the living room.

Rafe's truck. What the hell?

Lowering her gun, she took a peek through the peephole, just to make sure he was alone and then pulled open her door. "You scared the hell out of me," she told him. As her anger dissipated, at the tail end of the adrenaline the knock had sent searing through her, she wished she'd thought twice about opening her door.

The man was freshly showered. She could tell by the smell. In jeans that looked sinfully good on his lean, long legs, and a button-down blue shirt that was properly tailored to him, he'd definitely changed since she'd last seen him. His cowboy boots, a different pair from the day before, were equally flashy as those had been. He'd forgone the shave. And his blond bushy hair could have done with a brush.

"What do you want?" she asked. And then it occurred to her, he could be in trouble. Something could have happened.

"Are you okay?"

"No, I'm not okay, may I come in?"

"Of course." She stood back, let him in, glanced around outside, but nothing was out of place.

"What happened?" Thank God she'd already showered and dressed. She wanted time to get back up on Mustang Mountain after she'd finished her work for the day. Gun still in her hand, until she knew what they were dealing with, she led him into the dining room. Away from any windows anyone who'd followed him could shoot through.

"Nothing happened. There's no one out there," he told her, apparently having followed her gaze. "You can put the gun away."

Slowly, watching him, she did so. And realized her heart was pounding. "What's going on?"

"I would never ask you to ditch your family in order to be with me," he said, his tone kind of harsh.

That again. She'd thought they were done with it. Needed to be done with it.

And was touched that he'd obviously taken her words to heart to the point of showing up at her house disheveled—as disheveled as Rafe Colton ever got—at six in the morning. "It wasn't about you asking me, Rafe, it was about you including me."

It shouldn't matter that it was important to him. It really shouldn't.

They had to let go. Both of them. They just had to do it. Like ripping a bandage off a wound.

"I wasn't referring to twenty-three years ago," he said. She frowned. Had he been drinking?

She was pretty adept at discerning such things. Had a lifetime of experience doing so. Didn't see it in him. But…

"I don't get it," she said.

"I'm a Colton," he told her. "And you're asking me to leave my family in order to be with you."

What on earth? She frowned. "Rafe…" She started slowly, like she was speaking to someone who was confused. Because she was. "I never, ever asked you to leave your family. Or to be with me."

"No, you just tell me we can't be together, and the only reasoning you give, in your various ways, comes down to the fact that I'm a Colton."

He wanted to be with her? He *really* wanted to be with her? By the looks of him, he'd spent a great bit of the night stewing about the fact that she'd told him the day before that she wouldn't see him.

Because a Colton wasn't used to being told no? Didn't know how to accept a refusal?

Was it a matter of pride to him now?

Or did he really care?

"You being a Colton is what started our separation," she told him, needing to get the words right. To help them both understand. "But it's not what's keeping us apart."

Granted, she wouldn't be happy living in a mansion. But then, he didn't live in one. She'd never seen the house he'd built. On "their" land.

Because she'd meant that much to him.

But that was all beside the point.

"It's you, Rafe, and, probably me, too," she admitted. "Me, because I'm done. I've carried our love with me for decades, keeping it alive, only to find that all I was carrying was memories."

"How can you say that? Look at us. We've been back in contact four days and have hardly been separated since. And let me tell you, lady, that's not just because of the job we're doing together. I didn't hold you the other night because of the job. You weren't crying because of the job. You didn't climb down off that bed because of the job. And we most certainly didn't make incredible love, nine times, because of the job."

"You counted how many times we did it?"

And that mattered how in that moment?

She had to help him understand. Her sanity, and future happiness, depended on it. "We have a past, Rafe. A precious one that will always connect us and will always have the power to evoke emotions within us. But it's in the past."

"Because I'm a Colton."

"No. Because you weren't willing to fight for us, in spite of you being a Colton. Or me not being good enough for them. You let us go. Not just physically, but in your heart."

She saw the second her words hit home. It was like he'd been sucker punched. She stood there, physically watching reality dawn—in the drop of his shoulders, the shock in his gaze, the way the hand that had been outstretched to her dropped at his side.

It was almost done.

Chapter 22

Kerry was just getting ready to tell Rafe that the time had come for her to let him go from her heart, too, when there was another knock on her front door.

"What the hell!" She moved forward more quickly this time, but careful as always to take precautions. Another vehicle was out front, behind Rafe's truck. A somewhat new-looking white sedan. A glance through the peephole showed her a woman she'd never seen before, middle-aged, with graying hair, looking strung out.

Motioning to Rafe to get back into the dining room, behind the wall, waiting until he'd done so, she slowly pulled open the door, her gun ready to aim and fire.

"Detective Wilder?" the woman asked.

With her free hand she pointed to the badge already hooked to her belt. "Yes."

"My name's Lavinia Alvin. Grant Alvin was my husband." Looking more frightened than dangerous, the woman glanced behind her and, not sure she was making the right choice, Kerry let her in the house.

And then checked her for weapons the second she was in the door.

"I don't blame you for being careful," Lavinia told her. "I heard you've been asking around about your brother's death this past year, even though it was ruled an accident," she said. Standing in Kerry's foyer in jeans and wrinkled T-shirt, she had her lower lip sunken in as she spoke, and her thin, shoulder-length hair hanging around cheeks that were marked with a couple of scabs. "Tyler died just like my husband did," the woman said, surprisingly well-spoken.

Was Rafe listening?

The Rafe she'd known would be.

"Grant had some shady dealings," Lavinia said. "Started out to feed my habit. I got addicted to pain pills when I had my back surgery and just couldn't get off them. Too much pain, still," she added.

While she felt deeply sorry for the woman, a familiar feeling of excitement started to settle over Kerry. The cop's instinct that told her she was about to get her missing piece. Someone out to screw you didn't generally stand around and talk about their medical history.

Not with that genuine tone and unmistakable sorrow in eyes that were watery and looking straight at you.

"He was trying to break free," she said. "I'd been approved for a new surgery, but had to be clean to qualify for it. I'm supposed to be heading into a clinic next week. Grant was up on the mountain, getting rid of any evidence that could link him to what was going on up there. He was intending to tell them that he was quitting, that he wouldn't be following any more illegal orders, the night he was killed. He was going to put in for a leave from the forest service, too, so he could be in Tucson with me." Lips that hadn't been steady to begin with started to shake.

"Do you know what was going on up there?" Kerry asked. She had to stick to business. To help people by getting scum off their streets—and mountains. "Or who your husband worked for?"

Lavinia nodded, glanced behind her at the door, and around her, too. "Odin Rogers," she said, and everything inside Kerry went on alert.

She'd known. She'd been right.

But that meant Rogers wasn't just a two-bit slime that she suspected anymore. He was a real danger to Mountain Valley. A murderous threat.

"His real business is stockpiling weapons, but he runs drugs from across the border, too," Lavinia continued, her voice low, but her tone intense. "I wasn't going to say nothing, especially after Grant was killed, but he's watching me. Rogers and his goons. Everywhere I go, even outside my house, they're watching me."

Did that mean they were outside Kerry's home? Ready to strike?

"The only way I got away from them this time was by meeting my sister at the grocery, changing clothes with her and taking her car," she said. "She and her husband drove down from Phoenix to help me. She had another change of clothes for herself, not the ones she walked in with, and she put those on, with a hat, and her husband pulled up to the curb and she got in and they left. They called me when they were back out on the road, and waited to make sure I got away without being followed."

"Where are they now?"

"In nearby Mountain Valley, waiting to hear from me," Lavinia said. "But I'm not calling them. I'm not going to put them in any real danger. I just had to be able to get to you without Odin's people knowing, so you have a chance to do something about Odin and when my sister came up with the plan, I figured it would work without them getting hurt. I wanted to see you in person, wanted you to look me in the eye and know I'm telling the truth. Grant deserves that."

The woman was smart. Conscientious. Kerry wondered who she'd been, what she'd done, before a back injury had changed the course of her life.

Obviously she'd been someone who'd inspired Grant Alvin's love and loyalty. Kerry hadn't much liked the man, but she now knew why he'd wanted her and Rafe off the mountain.

"Do you have any idea where on the mountain they're holding their stash?" she asked next, already planning the phone calls she was about to make.

First and foremost, to get Lavinia Alvin into protective custody. The rest had waited two years. It could hold on a few more hours.

"I just know it's in an old mine," she said. "It used to be a working mine, a hundred years ago. It's near the middle of the mountain, away from the road, because Grant had to cover the area on foot. His job was to keep hikers and people like you away from it, and to run lookout when merchandise was going in or out. When they're moving guns, they use off-road vehicles to get them most of the way and then have to break them out of containers and carry them the rest of the way.

"Grant had to spend the night there once…he got caught up on the mountain when a monsoon hit. He said you go downhill to get in it, and then there's a flat area where the guns and drugs are stored. He slept down there with the guns. I thought they'd killed him then…" She shivered, and Kerry offered her a seat in the living room. Said she'd get her a sweater.

"A hoodie would be good, if you have one," the older woman said, and when Kerry grabbed one out of the closet just beyond them, Lavinia was still standing right there by the door.

At some point Odin's thugs were going to realize that Lavinia had slipped their watch. It would take some time. They'd have to look down every aisle in the grocery store first. But they'd get there.

And when they did…

"I have to go," Lavinia blurted. "They're going to figure out I'm gone and I don't want them to know I came here. They'll know they've been found out…"

"You can't go out there!" With a hand on the woman's shoulder, Kerry tried again to get her into the living room. "I'm going to make a phone call and get you into a safe house. Outside of Mustang Valley. I can ask the DA to provide police protection at all times, night and day, until we bring this guy in. But as a cop, I can tell you, you'll probably have it anyway. We need to stop this guy and we'll protect you on our own dime if that's what we need to do. No one else is going to die…"

She wanted Rafe out of there, too. Being on Odin Rogers's radar was like an infectious, terminal disease. No way could she bear the thought of it bringing Rafe down, too…

She let go of Lavinia to reach for her phone, and the other woman jerked at the front door. "Nowhere is safe for me," she said, and ran out.

Kerry turned to go after her but only got one step toward the door before two gunshots rang out, one after the other.

"Kerry!" Heart in his throat, Rafe ran from around the corner to see Kerry alive and running out the front door. Following her, he stopped himself from calling her name again. He needed to support her, not distract her.

Keeping himself covered by a half wall, a pillar attached to the overhang across her front door, he saw a black SUV pull away from the curb across the street and down one house. At the same time, Kerry darted out from behind the other pillar, gun drawn, and ran over to the body a few feet away.

He hadn't seen Lavinia Alvin, had only heard her voice, but he knew that the woman who was lying there with her eyes wide-open, and bleeding from the chest and the throat, had been the ranger's wife. Kerry's finger was pressed to the other side of the woman's neck.

"She's gone," she said, grabbing her phone and

pushing a speed dial. "Come on," she said, "give me your keys."

He didn't hesitate, just tossed them to her as they ran, and jumped into the passenger side of his own truck, whether or not she intended him to ride along.

She was armed. He wasn't.

He also wasn't sitting this one out.

"Chief, I've got a body outside my house," Kerry was saying into the phone, her voice even but also filled with urgency, as she broke speed limits. "Lavinia Alvin, wife of Grant Alvin. She just gave me the goods on Odin Rogers. I'm after the shooter. There are two of them in a black SUV..." She rattled off the license plate number. "I'm in Rafe Colton's truck. He's with me. I'll keep you posted." She disconnected the call immediately.

"You didn't wait for a response," Rafe said, holding the grab handle above his seat as he watched her race down her street and on to the next. With a couple of quick turns she took a shortcut out to the boulevard and got there just in time to see the SUV speed past them. "Hold on," Kerry said, and turned quickly to follow them.

As early as it was, there was little traffic out, for which Rafe was thankful. For their safety, but also for the citizens of Mustang Valley, who could be caught up in hell just for going about their daily lives.

He'd just heard a woman talking about her husband, about back surgery, grieving the second chance they'd almost had, and then seconds later had seen her lying dead on the ground, her blood draining out around her.

Not an everyday occurrence in his world.

The first time he'd ever been that close to a dead body, actually.

It could have been Kerry.

"They're headed out to the mountain," Kerry said. "They know we're right behind them so we can assume that they have plans to get rid of us out there."

He glanced over at her, hearing a different Kerry. A woman in complete control and capable of doing whatever it took to get her job done. She didn't seem the least bit fazed by the dead body she'd left behind on her front walk.

Not the Kerry he'd known at all.

"I'm going to stay close, but not too close, just in case one of them tries to take a shot at us out here on the road. I'd appreciate it if you stayed down, so you won't be a target."

"I'm not getting down," he said. "I'm going to watch your back."

"You need to watch your own."

"Are you kidding me?" he said, watching his side mirror to make certain there was no one coming up behind them. Odin had a crew. He could be planning an ambush greater than two against two. "We're in this together, Kerry. A couple. Facing the challenge together."

He knew he was slamming her. Right then and there. In the middle of what might lead to both their deaths, he was letting out the anger that had been slowly building inside him since he was five years old and had his life stripped away from him. She'd thought, all these years, that he hadn't had her back? "It's what I want to do and it's damn well what I'm going to do," he told her, adrenaline firing up his insides in a way all new to him.

She glanced his way, and then returned her focus fully to the road.

"Just be smart, and if I give you an order, you take it," she said. "I'm trained at this, Rafe. I know things you do not."

She knew a hell of a lot more than he did. About most things.

Too bad it took him thirty-six years to figure that out.

Grabbing the duffel that was still in his back seat—a guy never knew when he might need an extra toothbrush these days—he pulled out the tennis shoes he'd bought the other day. Took off his tie. Five-hundred-dollar pants paired with twenty-dollar tennis shoes didn't matter at the moment.

"You've got your gun in here, right?" she asked next.

"It's a hunting rifle." On the floor behind them.

"Is it loaded?"

"No, ammunition's in the glove box." He was already reaching for it.

"Get it loaded," she said. "But don't shoot unless you're in immediate danger," she said. "No matter what these guys have done, as a citizen, you can only shoot in self-defense, you got that?"

He got that she was worried about him. And he didn't want to distract her. "I've got it. I'm not going to go all commando on you and charge ahead, Kerry. You've got the lead here. I'm just your wingman. But I can guarantee you I'll be a good one. I'm not going to let you down."

He'd witnessed a woman go from talking to dead in

less than a minute. He and Kerry could die out there. He needed her to know where he stood.

His rifle was loaded. He prayed to God they wouldn't need it.

"The chief will have as many people out here as he can gather up," she said. "There's a posse in town who can pinch-hit as needed. Unfortunately, I don't have a radio, though, so we're going to be on our own in terms of intel."

He liked the first part, not the second. Wanted to know if she'd done something like this before

He didn't trust her any less. Just would worry about her more.

"There's a gravel road just before Mustang Mountain Drive," she was saying. "I'm going to pull in there. It leads up to the other side of the mountain, but then dead-ends. I'm assuming Rogers knows that. I want him to think that's where we're headed. He'll head us off from the other side. Then we'll double back and head up the road. I'm not giving him a chance to get back down off that mountain."

Rafe just cared about getting her off it.

In one piece.

Nothing else mattered. Not being a Colton or a Kay. Not money or oil or ranches, or even cops. All that mattered was her, Kerry Wilder, home, safe and happy.

Chapter 23

Kerry couldn't afford to be distracted. Not by Rafe's talk of facing challenges together—throwing back in her face what she'd accused him of not doing all of their lives.

Like he thought that a moment of danger on a case was enough to make up for letting go when the times got tough.

Danger was a blip in time. If you lived through it, that's when the hard part of living happened. The everyday, nonexciting, getting-up-and-doing-the-dishes stuff.

She turned off, saw the brief flash of red lights ahead as the driver of the SUV noticed them turning off. Slowing just enough on the gravel road to see that the SUV turned onto Mustang Mountain Drive, she waited to make certain that the vehicle wasn't coming back. No way was she going to get trapped on a dead-end road that no one knew she'd taken.

But if this worked…

Five minutes without sighting the SUV and she turned around, and then right, approached Mustang Mountain Drive slowly. She'd have liked for her backup to be there. Thought about waiting. But knew if she was just sitting out there when the SUV came back down off that mountain, she'd be dodging bullets. Without great odds.

She and Rafe would be sitting ducks to desperate men with a vehicle full of contraband. They'd die before they'd let themselves be caught.

And if she pulled back and waited?

They could pull right back off that mountain and get away with the goods.

She had to go up. But she didn't have to take Rafe with her.

She drove slowly, window down so she could listen for sounds of vehicles up ahead. Off-road or otherwise. The ground wasn't as smooth as it had been earlier in the week, indicating that there'd been some rain during the night. It happened. Especially in January. You'd get up in the morning, the desert ground would be dry, having greedily soaked up what moisture was there, but you'd smell the rain.

On the mountains, that same hardly noticeable storm could bring snow that would melt just as quickly, but leave the ground moist.

As they rounded a bend, the heavy truck's wheels spun for a second and then grabbed traction and continued forward. If she'd been in her Jeep, she wouldn't have had that problem.

"What do you want me to do?" Rafe asked, sitting beside her. That's when she had an idea. Pulling over in the next lay-by, she told him to get out.

"Stay low, out of sight," she said. "Wait for help to come and tell them what we know. I'm going to continue on up the road."

"I'm not leaving you."

She didn't have time to argue. Shouldn't have taken the time to stop at all, except having him down there, able to alert the chief or whomever came first, that she was up there had felt like a good plan.

Knowing he was safe was an even better one.

If she took too long deciding, the SUV could come right back down and trap them—run them off the road. It could turn into a shoot-out that most definitely wouldn't end well. Most particularly if they'd retrieved a stash of weapons.

She knew she was after Odin's people, but didn't know if he was with them.

She didn't just want them.

She was going to bring him in.

She was going to get Tyler—and now Grant and Lavinia Alvin—the justice they deserved.

Putting the truck in gear, she tried to back up. And then to move forward. Rafe told her to try low gear. He gave her a couple of other suggestions and every one of them just dug them in deeper. The truck was too heavy for the damp, dew-soaked earth.

"We're going to have to continue on foot," she told

him. "Find a place to hole up where they can't find us. Wait it out until the chief gets out here."

She didn't like the plan at all. Couldn't stand to feel like a sitting duck. Nor did she want to fail because of a truck in a ditch.

But she wasn't going to risk Rafe's life. Period.

Pulling out her phone she prayed for service, and was denied that blessing, as well.

"Come on," she said, getting out and closing her door softly behind her. Leading the way, she kept her body pressed to the mountain, gun out in front of her, and continued upward, Rafe right behind her. So close he was touching her.

Not holding on. Not pushing. Just there. In contact.

If she had to die, she couldn't think of a better way. On the job. Closing the most important case of her life. And touching Rafe.

Up until the part where if she died, and he was right there, probably so would he.

They climbed that way for fifteen minutes or more, taking each step quietly, placing their feet carefully, keeping the mountain as cover, slipping behind ridges that protected them from view of the road whenever they could.

Kerry didn't speak, and Rafe followed suit, just as he'd said he would.

At one point, when she turned her head to look behind them, bringing her face almost nose to nose with his, he leaned forward and kissed her. Not a peck. A deep, albeit quick, kiss. He didn't explain himself. She didn't ask questions. But it was like he'd given her some strange shot of energy.

A reason to go on. As if she needed one.

She was this close to getting Odin Rogers; she wasn't going to fail.

Kerry saw the SUV first. Of course, being in front, she would, but she stopped so suddenly his body pushed into hers. He held on. With the arm that wasn't holding his rifle, he held her back to his front, and looked where she was pointing, her gun in her hand. The SUV appeared to have veered off the road, with its front bumper protruding into the side of the mountain.

"Going too fast," Kerry said. Rafe agreed with her assessment. Was this a good sign that the men they were pursuing had crashed due to excessive speed?

"They could be hurt," he whispered back. Just wanting to stand there, holding her, until help arrived. Not out of fear for himself, but with every step she took out there, she risked losing her life. He just needed to know she was safe.

That's what she hadn't understood—twenty-three years ago, or even now, apparently. He loved her so much that protecting her mattered more than his own happiness—and still did.

"No one's slumped over the wheel. If they could move, they'd get out of there," she said softly. "They could be on the other side of the SUV. Come on." Taking his hand, she pushed him back the way they'd come until she could turn around and lead them both around the side of a hill and up, moving farther back into the mountain range as they climbed. Rafe watched her back, her front and all around them, prepared to use his rifle as a bat as much as anything. "We need a better vantage point," she said when they were far enough from the road to allow conversation.

Still, she kept her voice soft, almost a whisper. They had no idea how many people might be on the mountain. Or where.

Ten minutes more of mostly vertical hiking and they'd reached a small peak. Lying on her belly, Kerry pulled herself forward, gun in front of her nose, to the edge of the peak and looked downward.

She whispered, "I've got you, Odin." Four simple words. And filled with world-changing promise. That was the moment he understood just how completely Kerry meant what she said.

She couldn't believe it. She was lying flat on her belly, on cold mountain ground with the sun barely coming up on that cool January morning, and there below her, were two men—one gun visible, but she assumed they were both armed—standing at an open mouth in the earth.

Even more miraculous was that the man holding the gun was Odin Rogers. She had him.

She could take him out right then and right there. He'd never know what hit him. She could say it was self-defense.

She could…

Never do such a thing.

No way was the thug stealing her life away from her.

She'd found his mine.

She had him in her sights.

And now she had to figure out a way to get him in her cuffs.

"If we circle around down the other side of this peak, we should come out to the left of them. We could then circle back to come at them from behind. The advantage is ours because we know where they are and they have no idea where we are." Rafe's breath tickled the back of her neck as he lay beside her, leaning over to whisper close to her ear.

Probably no need to whisper, but the way sound traveled down, especially echoing in the mountains, she knew the call was a good one.

Never mind the shiver his breath sent through her. It kept her energized. Alive. Ready to move.

His idea was a good one. Except… "I don't think they plan to be there that long," she said. They were talking at least half an hour of hiking. Probably more. "Clearly Odin wants his thug to go down in the mine. Probably to stay down and guard the weapons. He wants them safe until he gets us off his trail. No way he could move them knowing that we're out here. And that we'd have called for backup." She'd understood the plan as soon as she'd seen them.

"Otherwise they'd be out looking for us," she finished. "Either he thinks that SUV is drivable, or he has another way out."

"Lavinia said they use off-road vehicles," Rafe said, as though reading her mind. "Could be they have one or two stashed out here."

Made perfect sense.

"And they'd be close to that mine," she said, searching the landscape for a sign of any place that could house a vehicle or two. The terrain was rough, but four-wheelers were made for that. If she could get down to the road, wait until the thug was safely underground and then confront Odin when he was trying to drive off…

It could work.

It *would* work.

"We've got to get down there," she said, pointing toward a curve in Mustang Mountain Drive just under where Odin and his man were standing. She couldn't actually see the drive from their vantage point, but she knew it was there.

Around a curve slightly on the other side of a mountain peak. They could be there in twenty minutes tops. She might not have that long.

She had to try. Checking for service, she saw one bar and handed her phone to Rafe. "Call the chief. Speed dial two. Let him know where to meet us. I'm starting down. You stay up here and watch my back."

She didn't wait for his reply. Didn't look at him, or consider the fact that she might not ever see him again.

She had to go.

Rafe watched Kerry get farther and farther away as he waited impatiently for her phone to connect. She'd left without even looking at him. Without a kiss for luck. Or a promise that she'd be fine. She'd left without telling him to be careful or stay safe.

She left without telling him she loved him—or letting him tell her.

It was like what they'd shared—the searching they'd been doing these past few days—hadn't mattered at all.

Just like she was trying to get him to believe that the past didn't matter anymore. She'd just walked away.

Put the job above all else.

Without giving him any say in their fate at all.

On one hand, he didn't blame her. Their safety was her job. Facing danger was her job. He'd opted to sign on, knowing there was danger. He'd jumped in his truck before she could drive off without him. It all made sense.

They were all sound decisions.

She hadn't even tried to connect with him one last time. Now all he could do was pray.

As her body moved in and out of view with the easy, stealthy movements she made, he watched her go knowing that she'd given up.

And he understood that, too.

It's exactly what he'd done twenty-three years ago.

Chapter 24

"Kerry, where are you?"

The phone had connected. Chief Barco's voice boomed in Rafe's ear. In as few words as possible, he described what was going on.

"She found the mine," he said, as soon as he'd explained that Kerry had taken off on her own and they needed backup as soon as possible. "We can't see what's inside it, but it's pretty clear that Odin Rogers has an intense stake in it." He told the chief Kerry's theory of what was going on below, and said, "Not clear why the guy isn't going down below, but he's clearly trying to convince Rogers of something. Lots of gesturing and pointing."

"Are they both armed?"

"You'd assume so," he said. "I can only see one gun." He answered Barco's questions succinctly.

"Are you armed?"

"With a hunting rifle."

"What's going on now?" He described the mine opening, the two men whose argument seemed to be heating up as Odin's thug looked down into the mine, shook his head and threw up a hand. The hand Rafe hadn't been able to see until then.

"They're both armed," he said. Kerry was already halfway down the vertical part of the climb. Would make it to the road in half the time he'd figured. He told the chief to hurry.

"Dane and I are almost there, and there are six others behind us," the chief said.

Townsmen who'd agreed to help search if need be. Kerry had already told him about them. He was told to stay where he was, to keep his eye on Kerry at all times. The chief deputized him over the phone. He had no idea if such a thing was even legal, or if the chief had meant him to take it that way, but he didn't care.

He had a sister who could sort all that out later, if need be.

After he rang off, he lay there on the ground, moving as necessary, to keep Kerry in sight. Praying he saw the chief before he saw Odin's thug enter the mine. Saw Odin leave.

And for one brief second he looked at something else, too.

The first number programmed in Kerry's speed dial was his.

Kerry was almost in position when all hell broke loose. She could hear two voices, Odin and his thug, she knew, but couldn't make out what they were saying. Their anger, however, was evident. They were getting desperate, and disagreeing. Not a good combination.

Because she'd done her job and put pressure on them.

Everyone made a mistake eventually. She'd heard it said often enough, in law enforcement circles, when talking about criminals who were hard to bring in.

Feeling a bit of a rush, knowing that she was at least somewhat complicit in Odin Rogers's making his error, she came around the edge of the cliff closest to them, her gun drawn, ready to announce herself and demand that they put the guns down. She didn't glance up at the cliff where she'd been. Didn't make certain that Rafe had her back with bullets that would travel the distance between them. She wasn't planning to give him a need to shoot.

She glanced again, just quickly, finalizing her plan, based on where the two were standing and obstructions in her path, just in case they didn't do as she demanded and drop their weapons.

"What was that?" She heard the words quite clearly. "You—you couldn't just get your ass in the hole like I told you…"

"I'm not goin' down there and I'm not goin' down for you, neither," the deep gruff voice came back.

A gunshot pierced the early morning air. And a split second later, another.

Pulse drumming through her, Kerry peeked around her ledge and saw Odin Rogers standing over his thug. And then, almost casually, the man turned and shot again, straight at her. She backed up, waited. Listened. Another shot rang out, from up above.

The cliff. Rafe.

He'd provided the second's worth of distraction she needed. Rounding the corner in that second, gun pointed, she saw that Odin had approached, was nearly upon her. But had turned to look up at the cliff.

And that's when she got him. Holding her gun to his neck, she grabbed one arm and twisted it back up behind him in a way that didn't take superior strength, just a knowledge of how to twist an arm so that any movement brought excruciating pain.

He fought her. She took an elbow to the chin. Scraped her shoulder on the side of the mountain. And delivered a knee to the small of his back, never letting go of the arm, or her gun at his neck.

"Drop your gun," she said through gritted teeth. And prayed that he did it. She didn't want to kill a man that day. And she wasn't going to lose this fight, either.

"You think you're so smart." Odin's breath stank as he turned his head to the side, as though trying to see her. "You don't know nothin', lady."

"I know you've got drugs and guns down in that mine. I know you killed Lavinia Alvin on my front porch this morning."

"I didn't kill that woman and whatever's in that mine, assuming somethin's there, ain't mine. I can't help it if Cane over there found 'em and told me about 'em. I ain't even seen 'em. I was just convincing him to call the cops when he pulled a gun on me."

She gave his arm another twist, for Tyler, ready

to crunch the slimy man's instep with the heel of her cowboy boot if he made any move at all.

"My brother said he wasn't going down for you and you shot him."

"You got no proof a that. And even if I did know about stuff down there, it ain't mine. Goods move in and out. That's how it works."

"I've got you, Rogers. Do yourself a favor and give it up."

"Don't matter even if I did. You ain't stoppin' nothin'. If it ain't one guy moving the goods, another will."

She moved again. Driving the pain she was inflicting deeper. She wasn't going to kill him, but if she broke his arm…

A car came barreling toward them. Chief Barco. Dane.

And as though on cue, Rafe came sliding down the hill, too. He had to have taken his shot and run, or had already been partially down before he shot.

"Drop the gun, Rogers," the chief said while he and Dane approached, both pointing their nine millimeters right at the criminal's head.

"You ain't gonna shoot with her right there behind me," he said. "But I might."

Odin lifted his gun and pulled the trigger just as another shot rang out. Kerry felt the power of the blast of shrapnel hitting Odin's gun, taking at least one of his fingers with it and exploding against the side of the mountain. A shot taken legally, in self-defense.

As Odin swore loudly, gruffly, Rafe stood there,

looking at his rifle like he didn't know what it had done. Or how it had done it.

Something else that had changed about him over the years. He'd improved his aim.

Dane and the chief moved in, Barco having to forcibly unbend Kerry's fingers from around Rogers's bent arm.

Odin Rogers stood there, his shot-up hand dripping blood while Dane slapped cuffs on him, and the chief wrapped a handkerchief around his wound.

"Good shot, Colton, but next time, leave the shooting to us. Got it?" Chief Barco said as he started to lead the greasy murderer away from her.

"Ha, I've still got the last laugh," Rogers spit out, turning to look at her. "Cane might've done most of the dirty work, thinkin' there at the end that he could squeeze me, but I'm the one who pushed your weak-assed weasel of a brother off that cliff. Him and the ranger, too."

The idiot had just confessed. In front of three law enforcement officers and a mostly innocent bystander.

Like she'd known the second she'd seen Odin standing at the opening to that mine—she had him, at long last.

Rafe asked for his keys and was glad when Kerry handed them over to him without an argument as one of the chief's officers arrived and drove them back to his truck. Dane had taken their prisoner into jail in the back of James's patrol car, as the chief was staying at the mine until ATF could get there and take possession of the drugs and weapons stashed inside it.

"I have to go into the station" were her first words to him once they were alone. Her first words to him period, other than asking him if he was all right.

He got it. She was working the scene. Had a job to do. Protocol to follow.

And she was avoiding…them.

It wasn't up to her to understand, or care, that he was still shaking from having shot at someone for the first time in his life. If he'd gone right, even a fraction…

"I've got reports to write."

"You can shower first. Clean up."

"I already showered this morning and I'm fine," she told him.

"Your Jeep is at your place."

"Lizzie can run me home at lunch. Seriously, Rafe, I get that this morning was out of the norm for you and it's not like I'm facing down guns on a regular basis, but this is my job. This is what I do. And now I have to go write it up. Besides, if you think I'm going to miss one second of Odin Rogers's interrogation…"

She was fired up. And covering up, too. She wouldn't look at him. Didn't even seem to see him, other than as the body that had helped get his truck out of the mud and was now driving the vehicle them both back to town.

While he was needing her. And he needed to say things *to* her.

"You'll need to come in, too," she said. "Long enough to give a statement. Not to me. You'll need to speak with Dane. I'll make sure he gets to you first so you can get on to your day."

So saying, she picked up her phone, dialed and was clearly speaking to her fellow detective as she gave her location and arranged to have Rafe present and ready for questioning in twenty minutes. About the time it was going to take for them to get to the station, park and get inside.

Not a minute to spare.

Without speaking to him first about it. As though she was the boss.

Which, he had to acknowledge, she probably was. He'd jumped into the investigation. He'd shot a man's finger off. Realizing that Kerry was taking care of him as well as doing her job, he sat back and drove her into town.

Mustang Valley Boulevard was coming to life as he pulled into town and it was odd to think that a lot of people were just having breakfast. He felt as though he'd lived a day and a half, at least, since he'd rolled out of bed that morning.

When he parked in a visitor's slot at the police station, Kerry reached for the door handle immediately, but he held her back with a hand on her arm. She stilled, sitting there, staring toward the dash.

He waited until she looked him in the eye.

"We aren't done yet," he said. "If nothing else we have to figure out how we go back to coexisting in the same town and stay away from each other." If nothing else. But there was something else. He just needed a minute to figure out what it was. And what to do with it.

She pursed her lips, her chin tight. But, still looking at him, finally nodded.

He couldn't stop staring at her. Couldn't stop the flood of gratitude that she'd made it off the mountain without injury.

"Congratulations, Ker, you got him," he said, all the love he felt for the woman pouring out in his voice.

Her lower lip started to tremble and she bit it. Nodded, and got out of the truck.

Rafe followed her inside.

On an adrenaline high, Kerry managed to stay focused on work the rest of that morning. Two years' worth of investigating—of sometimes being the only one believing there might be a case in her brother's death, of pressing forward when everything pointed against her success, of spending evenings and weekends sticking things to her dining room wall and staring at them—had finally come to fruition. Everyone, from the mayor who stopped in, the chief and all of her coworkers, congratulated her. Invited her out for drinks. People in town who'd lived under the shadow of Odin Rogers, whose kids had been sucked in by the drugs he peddled, and those who'd feared their kids would be sucked in—including the high school principal—stopped in or called as the news quickly spread about the police action out on Mustang Mountain early that morning.

She sat and listened as Odin Rogers was questioned, and tried to make a deal in exchange for turning in his suppliers. And she nodded as the chief got names out of him, without any deal on the table. Rogers had been a menace to their small town for too long to be allowed to walk free.

She'd seen Rafe in with Dane. And she'd seen him leave.

And she discovered that Grayson Colton had a rock-solid alibi for the night of Payne's shooting. The first responder Colton had been on a call—a car wreck with a fatality involved. The report was already in the police database and came up as soon as she typed in his name.

At lunchtime, after Lizzie took her to get her car, she went to the cemetery with a take-out piece of carrot cake and a chocolate chip cookie from the diner. She set the first on Tyler Sr.'s grave and the second on Tyler Jr.'s.

Yeah, wildlife would eat them, sooner rather than later, but she delivered anyway. Whispered her love. And went back to her Jeep.

That was when she fell apart. Sobbing, aching all over, inside and out, she cried. For her father's broken heart, her mother's broken dreams, her brother's broken life. She cried because she hadn't been able to save any of them.

And she cried because it was over. She'd gotten what she so badly needed, what she'd spent two years of her life to get, and in so doing, had just lost the last reason for Rafe to be in her life. He'd atoned for any wrong he'd done Tyler

Atoned and then some.

Thinking of his last act on the mountaintop that morning, she smiled through her tears. The man was one hell of a shot. A hotshot, too. Dane had been about to deliver the bullet that would have disarmed Odin, but it probably wouldn't have been so impressive.

The Colton heir had also been there for her, risking his life to see that she got the justice she needed. How did a girl walk away from that?

She'd have to be pretty dumb to do so, wouldn't she?

He'd said they weren't done yet.

She'd wanted to say, "Yes, we are," that morning in his truck, but the words wouldn't come.

He wanted to be friends. To stay in touch.

He was offering her what he had to give now. So how would she be any different than he'd been twenty-three years before, or when they both returned from college and he never got in touch, if she ignored his efforts to find a way to make them work?

So they wouldn't be married and live together for happily-ever-after. They could still have each other's backs. Fight injustices.

Maybe they could even make love once in a while. Unless that got too complicated.

Or she could go back to just being a cop. It would hurt a lot less.

The idea wasn't all bad.

Was actually kind of tempting.

Wiping her tears away, Kerry blew her nose and started the Jeep. She had a good life. A stable one, which was something she hadn't known growing up.

She didn't live with insecurity anymore. Or with anyone who worshipped substances more than the people they loved.

And she didn't live with the fear or worry of ever losing a loved one again. She just wasn't sure she could do that again.

It had taken twenty-three years for her to be in a

place where she was content. Where pain and loss weren't constant companions.

She'd been grieving since she was a little kid. Ever since she could remember.

She'd lost everyone. First her mom, right after Tyler was born. Rafe, at thirteen. Then her dad. And, two years before, Tyler. Add to that dealing with her Dad's drinking and Tyler's drugs in between—it was enough agony for a lifetime.

Chapter 25

As soon as he'd finished with Dane, Rafe phoned Genevieve to say he'd be late for his shift and went home to shower again. His five-hundred-dollar pants went in the trash. The cheap tennis shoes, he tucked away on the top shelf in a corner of his walk-in closet.

He had some coffee, made a couple of business calls and then headed back into town. To the hospital, first. Up to Payne's room.

Callum was there, with Genevieve. Grayson had just left—Rafe had passed him in the hall downstairs. "Hey," his lone wolf brother said as he stopped him. "What's going on, man? You okay? I heard something come through on the radio. A call for a bus on standby…"

As the owner of his own first responder agency

that aided police, firefighters and EMTs, Grayson was privy to anything that went out on police radio communications.

"I shot a guy's finger off this morning," Rafe said, when his normal inclination would have been to brush the whole thing off and move on. He wasn't one to spill his beans to the rest of the family. His role was to be responsible, to help them, not to bring them his problems.

"You're the one who fired the shot that knocked the gun out of that bastard's hand?"

One thing about Mustang Valley: word traveled fast. Of course, Grayson was on the pipeline pretty much 24-7. The man didn't seem to give a hoot about Colton Oil, but he cared deeply about helping others.

"All that shooting at the range," he said, referring to days when Payne would cart off the boys and make them stand at targets and shoot until he was satisfied that they could all defend themselves, or each other, if the need ever arose.

Having money made them targets, he'd told them.

Could have had something to do with the reason Callum had become a Navy SEAL and then an elite bodyguard, Grayson a first responder. They might not be following in Payne's footsteps or choosing the path he'd have chosen for them. But they were products of his teachings, just the same.

"Just glad you're okay, man," Grayson said. "I'm on my way out, but I want to hear about how you ended up on the mountain in the first place," he called back as he headed down the hall.

He was going to have to answer to the family. He knew that.

But first things first. Genevieve and Callum were waiting for him.

"Can I have a few minutes alone with him?" he asked after hearing the night's report. No change. Again.

Callum offered to take his mother out to breakfast and home to shower and rest. Ainsley was due in shortly.

And then he was alone with the man who'd shaped pretty much his entire life.

Pulling a chair up close, Rafe leaned his elbows on his knees and looked at the craggy, weathered features that he'd at times both revered and feared.

"We need to talk," he said. "And before you start to take control of the conversation, I have to tell you that I'm just not open to that this time around."

The doctor had said there was every chance the man could hear them. He wasn't going to coddle him because he was lying in a bed.

Chances were, knowing Payne Colton, he'd rejoin them only when he was ready.

And would not only remember all the conversations that went on around him, but would hold others accountable for them, too.

"When I was eight years old, you brought me into your study to tell me that I had to call you something. That it wasn't right that I never referred to you by a name, or called you a name. That you had to be someone to me. At the time, you told me that you wanted me to call you Dad, like the rest of the Colton children under your roof. But you gave me the option not to do so," he said, remembering those moments so clearly.

"It was one of the few times you actually gave me a choice, about anything, in my life. You know, my memories of my own father have faded some over the years, but one thing I remember clearly is that he always involved me in the decisions that affected our little family. So, yeah, looking back, maybe he was posing the situation to me in a way that would lead me to the decision he wanted me to make, but the point was, I always felt like I was consulted. That I had choices. And then, once made, I had to be accountable for them."

He stopped. Took a second to regroup. He was getting off track. Seemed once he'd realized—up on the mountain that morning, lying on his belly, watching the love of his life approach a known murderer—that he had some things to say, he'd given mental permission for a whole floodgate to open.

"I chose not to call you Dad," he continued when his mind was clear again. "You said then that I had to call you 'sir.'"

He stopped. Swallowed. Looked at that old face and felt a moment of fear. Fear that the man who'd raised and cared for him, who'd given him a place at his table and a seat on his board, wouldn't wake up.

"Art, food, the finer things…you gave it all to me," he said. "And I ate it all up. Developed a healthy appetite for all of it." He'd perfected traveling the world as a member of the young, elite wealthy. "But I've recently been reminded of the man I started out to be…the man I was growing up to be until my father died and the choices were taken away from me. And I discovered that there's no *thing* on this earth that's as moving or beautiful as moments with someone you love. Food really does taste better when it's shared with someone you love. Makes no scientific sense, doesn't add up or calculate, but that's my truth and I stand by it."

Off track again.

He looked at his hands. Took a deep breath. Looked back at the man who'd shown no sign of life for days other than the rise and fall of his chest as he breathed. No twitches. No change of the stoic expression.

Maybe Payne was just tired. Needed some rest. So that he could wake up and spend the next twenty years ruling over them all. Getting his way.

Rafe had a specific purpose. Someplace he was supposed to get with all of this discussion. Had thought, on his way in, that he'd be there in a couple of sentences.

"I had this thought that I would be disloyal to my father if I called you Dad," he confessed. "That it would be dishonoring him. Replacing him, even. But I never called him Dad. He died when he was still 'Daddy' to me.

"So here's the thing, sir. I'm grateful to you, indebted to you. You've given me a family, siblings, a life that I value…" No…that wasn't it…

"I…just… I'm going to be more like the rest of the Colton siblings from now on," he said. "I'm going to make the choices I need to make to be the person I'm meant to be. The person you—and my father—raised me to be. A man who lives authentically."

There.

Wow.

Yeah, that was it.

And...

His chin tightened.

"And... I love you, Dad."

Kerry left work on time that night. It had been one hell of a long day. A long week. She still had some small leads to follow on the Colton case, but until another clue broke free, until she found something, until someone came forward, or something else happened, there was nothing pressing, requiring her immediate focus.

Other than Ace, all of the Colton siblings now had alibis for the night of the shooting. The shooter had been male, according to Joanne's eyewitness account, which automatically knocked out Marlowe and Ainsley. Rafe and Asher had been at the mansion. Callum was on a job out of town. And Grayson had been at the scene of a car accident. That left Ace.

She had more investigating to do into his background. Going back to when he was young and lost his mother. Maybe trying to find some schoolteachers who might be able to give her some insights into how he took his father's second marriage. Spencer wasn't close with the family, but maybe he could give her some insights.

And she wasn't giving up on Nan Gelman. The woman existed, by whatever name, and Kerry wouldn't stop until she found her.

Whoever the shooter was should take note.

She was tenacious. She exerted her power quietly,

simply by not giving up. Odin Rogers was testimony to that.

She was going to find out who shot Payne Colton. And she would bring the man to justice.

Period.

In the meantime, she wanted to go home. To sit. To be.

And to figure out how Rafe Colton fit into her future. Not how he might want to fit. But how she wanted him to fit.

If at all.

This time the choice was going to be hers.

She was determined. And knew that not only could she take care of herself, she deserved to take care of herself.

Turning onto her street, she felt better than she had all afternoon.

She was strong. Capable.

She could choose who to love. Or how to love.

Or not to love.

His truck was in her driveway. He hadn't called. Hadn't asked if he could be in her space.

He was blocking her garage.

And before she could deal with any of it, she, damned fool, started to cry again.

All afternoon she'd been preparing not to see him again. At least not immediately. Not at her house, where she'd been allowed to hold him. To make love with him.

To be held by him.

She needed to keep going, drive on past. But couldn't see clearly through her tears. Stopping the

Jeep out front, just so she could grab a tissue, she was busy searching for one when there was a knock on her door.

She opened it. As one did.

Rafe reached over, put her vehicle in gear. Unbelted her.

And she let him. Like some kind of helpless little girl.

The girl she'd been.

The girl she'd never be again.

"What's wrong?" he asked, sounding scared. Worried. "Are you hurt? What happened?"

And she realized… He didn't know she was falling apart because of him.

And there was something she hadn't known, either. Seeing him there, right when she was falling apart… she had to face the truth about herself.

"I don't care what job I have, or where I live…if I have you," she said, still crying, but getting the words out clearly. "I just don't care, Rafe. If my hair's long or short, if I'm in Arizona or Alaska, in a small town or big city…none of it matters to me as much as being with the one person in the world I love more than I've ever loved anyone. I thought it would go away. I thought it would change.

"I thought I had a choice…" The last broke off on a sob and she was in his arms, holding on to him, letting it all out. "You left me…"

"I don't think I did."

His words reached her and she pulled back to stare at him. Seriously? He didn't get it?

"Can we go inside?" he asked. "Have this conversation in private?"

Glancing around, she didn't see anyone out in their yards. And cars driving by—there was one, but it would move on down the road.

"No," she said. She couldn't have him in again, just to watch him walk away.

"Have it your way." Moving them out of the road, he took her hand and started to walk with her, to the sidewalk, and then down the street. "I didn't leave you, Ker, not in the way you think. My heart never stopped loving you, not for one second. It damn sure never let you go. What I did do was hide. Not at first. When I was a kid, I did what I had to do, as far as I understood, to be a good person. And…to take care of me. I didn't tell you about Payne's ultimatum to protect you and your family. But also to protect myself. I couldn't bear the thought of you moving away, of not having you close, of not being able to watch you through my window…"

They reached a crosswalk, took it and headed back toward her house on the other side of the street.

"But later, when I reached adulthood, I thought I was beyond my youth, all grown-up, and ready to come home, take up the reins I'd been given at Colton Oil and face the fact that you'd never be close again. And then I get back and hear that you're home, too. And a cop. Right here in town. That's when I screwed up. I was healthy. Enjoying the good life. I felt carefree. Capable. I'd grown out of the young boy who'd been so lonely, who'd spent so many hours watching you from his window. Payne Colton, in giving me everything, had also stripped everything that I'd been from me. Living without was easier, because I could hide it in being a part of something important, a part of the Colton legacy and the influence that gave me. Living the high life was nice, too."

She listened so hard she was barely aware of the sky above. The houses up from the curb. The cool air. It was like he was inside her again, a place she'd once taken for granted. There was no judgment. It was how they used to be. Able to tell each other anything and know it would be okay.

Because it came with another knowledge—that no matter what was said, or what happened, nothing would ever separate them. Their love was that strong.

For so many years she'd tried to understand how that had all been a lie. To deal with the loss. To live without him.

Instead, she'd moved back to town because he was close. She'd never even cut her hair...

"But I never stopped loving you, Ker. I think I tried, on some level, at least. I lost touch with the self I'd started out to be. The self with whom I've become re-acquainted with this week. The self I've had to face with shame. I was selfish, Kerry. And weak. Afraid of ever hurting again as much as it hurt when I had to quit seeing you...but I always loved you. In my deepest whatever, it's always you. Always has been. Always will be."

Squeezing his fingers so tightly her hand hurt, she smiled. Walked. Cried some. It was like they'd left the sidewalk, left Mustang Valley, and were up with the clouds, in the no-man's-land that had once been their friendship.

"I'm also a Colton," he said. "And I love my family."

"I know," she said, sniffling.

"So…we have a challenge in front of us," he continued, and she loved the break in his voice almost as much as she loved him. "I'm bringing it to you this time, Ker. How do we make this work?"

And she was back on the sidewalk, passing her house across the street, continuing on down the road.

"I don't know." He couldn't just move away and never look back like she could. It was easy for her to say she'd live anywhere. She had no one else who really needed her. No one else she loved.

"I do."

His words stopped her in their tracks. Pulling something out of his pocket, he held it out. A ring, with the biggest diamond she'd ever seen. And then, kneeling in front of her, he looked up to the sky. To the mothers. And back at her. "Kerry Ann Wilder, will you marry me?"

She blinked. Felt her heart pounding. Needed to cry. Couldn't move. "Rafe…" He was sweet and dear, and hers, she got that now, but…

"Stand up," she said. And while she was disappointed when he did, she knew it was the right thing.

"We need to talk about this," she said. "You need to talk to Payne—" she remembered, of course, that he couldn't do that, and quickly changed it "—your family…"

"I am a Colton," he told her, shaking his head. "And

Coltons do what they need to do. I need to do this, Kerry."

"But…how would it work? Where would we live? And, my job…"

"We're both going to have to make sacrifices," he told her. "I'm expecting it's not going to be easy sometimes. We might even have our first fight…"

"Oh, not our first one," she said, shaking all over. "Remember the time you tripped me so you could grab the Easter egg I'd found first?" They couldn't have been more than five. His dad had still been alive.

"What I remember most is that I've loved you my whole life, Ker. I'd like us to live at my house, but if you can't bear to be back at the ranch, we'll figure out something. Ace has a place in town. So do some of the others…"

She looked at the ring he still held. Wanted it so badly she ached. "But what about your family? What about Payne?"

"The rest of the Colton siblings aren't likely to blink more than once or twice and then welcome you in. Genevieve might take some convincing, but she always comes around. And Dad, the worst he can do is disown me, and then our lives will change again. Like I said, it isn't going to be easy, but a smart woman I know pointed out that nothing else matters if we can be together." He kissed her. She wanted to hold on to those lips as she kept hearing the word *Dad*. Breaking away, she looked up at him.

Half-afraid he'd lost his mind. Or she had.

"We have to try to make it work, Kerry. Frankly, a love that stays alive over twenty-three years of stupidity and stubbornness, and then pulls us back together so completely, isn't something I'm willing to turn my back on. How about you?"

She knew now he had opened his heart to Payne Colton. Because he couldn't open fully to her unless he did so. No more hiding away. No more blocking the things he felt.

"Yes, Rafe Colton, I'll marry you," she said, ignoring the enormous diamond in his hand to throw her arms around his neck and kiss him. Hard. Deep.

Just like their journey to find each other again had been.

And when he finally pulled back to slide the ring on her finger, she heard the soft hailing of the small crowd of neighbors who'd been gathering a short distance away, to cheer on the cop who'd spent so many years keeping them all safe.

She wasn't alone anymore.

Because she'd finally dared to fully open her own heart to the town and to the man who'd always, in their own ways, had her back—and loved her in return.

* * * * *

Don't miss book one in
The Coltons of Mustang Valley series,
Colton Baby Conspiracy *by Marie Ferrarella.*
Available now wherever
Harlequin Romantic Suspense books are sold.

And check out the next two volumes,
Colton Family Bodyguard *by Jennifer Morey*
and
Colton First Responder *by Linda O. Johnston,*
Both available in February 2020!

WE HOPE YOU ENJOYED THIS BOOK!

HARLEQUIN®

ROMANTIC suspense

Experience the rush of thrilling adventure, captivating mystery and unexpected romance.

Discover four new books every month, available wherever books are sold!

Harlequin.com

Love Harlequin romance?

DISCOVER.

Be the first to find out about promotions, news and exclusive content!

Facebook.com/HarlequinBooks

Twitter.com/HarlequinBooks

Instagram.com/HarlequinBooks

Pinterest.com/HarlequinBooks

ReaderService.com

EXPLORE.

Sign up for the Harlequin e-newsletter and download a free book from any series at **TryHarlequin.com.**

CONNECT.

Join our Harlequin community to share your thoughts and connect with other romance readers!
Facebook.com/groups/HarlequinConnection

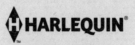

HARLEQUIN®

**ROMANCE WHEN
YOU NEED IT**

HSOCIAL2018